Canongate to Cannon Shell

Canongate to Cannon Shell

A Compilation of Stories and Poetry

G.B. Carmichael

Lineage Independent Publishing

Marriottsville, MD

To 26483 Private Gabriel Baird Carmichael. You are never forgotten.

Gabriel Baird Carmichael, the author's great-uncle, was born in Polmont, Stirlingshire, Scotland. He served in France with the 2nd Battalion, Argyll and Sutherland Highlanders. He was wounded on October 23, 1918 and died of his wounds on October 25, 1918 – slightly more than a fortnight before the Armistice, "at the eleventh hour on the eleventh day of the eleventh month of 1918." Private Carmichael is buried in Premont British Cemetery, France.

Gabriel Baird Carmichael

Contents

Foreword

Patricia Donoghue, writing under the *nom de plume* of G.B. Carmichael, and I have never met. Regardless, the bond between writers seems to transcend all distances, even the breadth of the ocean that is between us. We first became acquainted with each other through social media and a mutual friend – who insisted that I, as an independent publisher and mentor to other emerging authors, take a look at Pat's work.

What I discovered were stories full of feeling, emotive language, and visual images that tugged at my heartstrings. She writes about her perceptions of the visceral experiences of those affected by military conflict, going as far back as World War I. She writes about disasters that took place in the UK and elsewhere. She writes about... well... to tell you more would spoil the story lines!

As an added bonus, Pat has also included a couple of her poems and four novellas. Each of her works in this compilation drew me into the stories and into the lives of her characters – to the point that I was at times absorbed into the stories and distracted from the process of editing and formatting.

We also had to deal with the idiosyncrasies of British vs. American English. As George Bernard Shaw put it, "two countries separated by the same language." There are differences in spelling, differences in punctuation, and even differences in word meanings that we simply had to talk through. Regardless, the book is Patricia's, so the "Queen's English" won out – except for punctuation of dialogue.

I truly hope that this is not the only book that I publish with either Pat's true name or *nom de plume*. In fact, I have heard a rumor – from a qualified source – that at least one full-length novel is already in the works and that a second is floating around in the creative spaces of her mind. I hope, after reading this compilation of her works to date, that you, too, will look forward to her future releases.

Michael Paul Hurd
Editor/Publisher
Lineage Independent Publishing

Now I am Old

Now I am old, my thoughts are mostly spent revisiting the past as opposed to imagining what little future there may be left. And please, dear reader, do not think I am melancholic at the idea of my approaching demise. Since childhood, death has held no terror laden thoughts for me. The manner of my passing is of some interest, but only in as much as I'd like it to be as pain free as possible. There are some deaths that do fill me with horror, but that is another story for another day.

Today, I shall deal with one episode where I experienced fear at a level I wouldn't wish on anyone, even those perpetrators who brought hell to my life and fear to my heart. Echoes of that day are with me now. In all my senses I see their faces, smell my sweat, taste the bile as it rose in my throat, feel the trembling of my knees, and I can hear the click as the safety came off our weapons.

Allow me to walk you through my descent into a world of hatred, bigotry, and bloodshed.

It is 1973 on a cold, windy, wild January day in Crossmaglen, Northern Ireland. We are walking in a diamond formation down a beautiful country lane. Intel had come in earlier in the morning from a local driver who reported seeing a group of men on a quiet lane when on his way in to pick up his load before setting off for the day's deliveries. Him being an Orangeman, and all for Her Majesty's troops, he thought to tip them the wink, to keep an eye out for trouble on that stretch of road. He was thanked for the intel, and he left the sanger and disappeared off the face of the earth, though we didn't know that then. We later discovered he'd flown to Boston that morning at 11.30am, after landing there, he disappeared from all official records.

A Company, that's us, were assigned to go and investigate the report. There were six of us. Me, Troopers, Steve Little, Andy Manktelow, Dave Smith, Lance Cpl Ian Blackie and Sgt, Rene Villiers, aka, Killer, Bucket mouth, Adonis, Nig, Frenchie and me, Pill

We were all very verbal, teasing and taking the mick out of each other, it covered our anxiety. Going into bandit country was never just a pleasant drive through the beautiful countryside. It was fraught with a variety of ways to die. Ambushes, IEDs (*improvised explosive devices*) and snipers. No-one ever wanted to be sent out on one of these shouts.

Anyway, there we were strolling down a long narrow road that rose from a bend and curled up and left. We'd had to leave our armoured vehicle at the bottom or else we'd have blocked the road.

As I said, we are in diamond formation. I am in the rear position, Killer and Bucket-mouth are ahead left and right, with Adonis and Nig also left and right about 5yds further ahead and Frenchie is our tip of the sword. I'm walking backwards and only turn to face the front if one of the guys have eyes on rear, and only so that I can see where the road is heading. We were now very quiet, and the tension palpable. It was very stressful, walking in the glorious green countryside of Armagh back in the 70s, especially if you were a squaddie or a member of the R.U.C. (Royal Ulster Constabulary)

The front three had stopped at the point on our maps indicated by the driver, we three in the rear held our positions. Too late we noticed the old caravan just up ahead.

3

In less time than it took Frenchie to yell a warning, the door flew open and a hail of bullets poured forth inviting us to hit the decks pretty damn sharpish. At what seemed the same moment, a group of about a dozen men came from the tree line to our left. Rene yelled, "everyone, back to the pig!" (*that was our vehicle, our armoured Humber Pig*). It would be our only hope! Rene yelled again, "run, come on, run ya bastards!" He turned, firing from the hip as he shoved a stunned Nig into a run. In what was really only a heartbeat, but felt oh so much longer, we all finally burst into action. You might think I should be the first back, me bringing up the rear like, but that's not how it works.

I dropped to one knee and gave covering fire for those up front as they raced toward the Pig. Frenchie has just about reached the cab door when a bullet catches him in the shoulder and spins him away from the door and he falls to his knees. His rifle at his feet having fallen from his useless fingers. But he's yelling, "come on guys, get back here."

There's no cover to use, the odd bush or shrub, I see Dave smile as he races past me, then I hear a thud and a grunt as he catches a bullet too. It must have been a dum-dum bullet as there's a hole the size of a melon in his back, the contents of said hole were splattered all over me! I ran to him, scrabbling for my field dressing pack on my belt, but as I reach him, I can see from his eyes, he's gone, I check his pulse to be certain. I confirm we are a man down.

Before there was time to register that I'd lost a friend, Ian reaches me, and between us we drag Dave back to the Pig. Rene and Andy are grappling with Dave's body and Andy's firing over Rene's shoulder as they load the dead and injured into the back. I can feel the whoosh of bullets as they zing past me, my knees have gone to jelly, my mouth is dry, my palms are sweating, and I'm cold.

Everything seems to slow down. I notice a wee rabbit on the grass to my left dive down into his warren. I note the warmth of the sun.

At last, it seems Rene and Steve are now in the back, Andy and I are giving covering fire as Ian jumps into the driver seat. Andy throws himself into the back and I'm piling into the now accelerating Pig. Ian is reversing at speed, attempting to get us out of range. We hear the 'ting' of small arms fire hitting the bodywork. We are about 500yds away from them when Ian pulls his infamous hand-brake turn, then we really are speeding along the roads. Dave's body on the floor between our feet give us pause and restrains our urge to whoop and holler in celebration of our survival.

Rene is still bleeding a bit, but he is vocalising his pain in fine colourful language, so that's a good sign. We stop about five miles down the road, and as one, we exit the vehicle and vomit. This now joins the urine, blood and bone that decorate my uniform. I have to fight the urge to tear it all from my body in horror of having Dave as some psychedelic pattern on my jacket! We are all cold, shivering, and shaken as we mount up and return to Sanger Barracks and safety.

Our first taste of enemy contact, it's 1-0 to them, such a loss for us. Adonis was a big part of our life, had been since training at Bovington. We had lost an important member of our team, but more importantly, we had lost a friend. We were the bearers to carry Dave onto and off the plane taking us to Brize Norton then on to Dave's hometown. We'd again be his bearers at his full military burial, he would have done the same for any one of us, and we all knew that it could just as easily have been us.

Even today, over forty years later, a backfiring car can put me right back on that Armagh country road, the only time in adult life that I lost control of my bladder. We encountered contact with enemy forces more than once in Ireland and other hot spots around the globe, but I was never as afraid as I was that day.

And now that I am old, the only thing that frightens me is that I might live too long.

Photo by Christian Birkholz from Pixabay

The Rifles

I have watched,
and I have wept.
As Wootton's saddest
Vigil's kept.

I have seen the faces,
of those heroes of today.
And wonder at the courage,
and the sacrifice they pay.

Whilst sorrow fills my heart,
for those families bereft.
I share a moments pride,
with all those who are left.

And I'm filled to overflowing,
with such gratitude to all,
who serve and stand, and
offer, to stand and fight or fall.

So today I'm saying thank you,

to every serving member,

but especially tell the Rifles,

here's one who will remember.

Photo by Robert Pender from Pixabay

Revenge is Mine

Eleanor stepped off the plane; the Iraqi heat was oppressive.

Dressed in a long-sleeved lemon shirt and navy linen trousers, she moved down the steps with long, loping strides. She was 5' 9" with high, sharp, cheek bones. Not beautiful in the accepted sense, but attractive in an elegant, ethereal way. Large green eyes, a strawberry blonde and skin like rose-tinted alabaster. She looked like most European women visitors to the most inhospitable place in the world.

She had flown from Paris, ostensibly to meet with the head of the antiquities department to discuss a possible archaeological dig. It would be an important discussion, but neither she, nor the Paris Museum, believed they would get a permit. But then, that wasn't her primary reason for being there.

As she proceeded through customs she smoothed her hand over her left eye lid, it twitched when she was anxious. She was ushered through by officials who made no secret of their contempt for European women and her wild uncovered blonde curls. She pulled her scarf from her bag and covered her head and neck before moving into the baggage collection area. The man waiting, as she emerged having collected her small steel antler case, was Sa'id. They'd met years before at Cambridge, where they were on the same archaeology degree course, she worked in Arabic antiquities in Paris, and he was now head of the department for antiquities in the Iraqi government.

As soon as they stepped outside, both the heat and the noise hit her in a physical way, like an explosive wave, she hated it. Both the environment of distrust and noise, and the heat especially. It asked so much more from her than the same job in any European country.

Her son, Rhodri, had wanted to come with her on this trip, but this wasn't a sightseeing trip. She had another job - the reason she was here - to bring down gun runners.

Rhodri was disappointed and he'd still been cool with her when she dropped him at her brother Iain's house in Callander. Eleanor's mother had moved her and her sibling there from Stirling where she was born after the death of her father, when she was eleven. Only her brother had stayed local, he was a passionate Scot who loved his homeland. And in 2006 - after 5 years in the Argyll's - he was standing as SNP candidate for Callander. He had his own advertising web business, promoting Scotland in all her guises to the world.

Iain was the eldest sibling. James, her junior, was with Greenpeace somewhere near Resolute and the north-west passage in Canada. Aileen, her big sister, was in Virginia, USA, her husband was in law enforcement, and she was a forensic pathologist. Her son and Iain had been close since Rhodri's birth eight years ago, and he was the only one who knew who her son's father was. Her son hero-worshipped his ex-soldier uncle who served in many of the modern-day war zones, including Iraq, which was another reason Eleanor had accepted this assignment.

Jeff had been Iain's best friend and Rhodri's dad. A large number of illegally trafficked guns had made their way into the insurgent's hands in the same area their unit had been posted in 2004. An IED was reported by the lead vehicle and Jeff was next up on the rota to defuse any devices found. He had done his job well and made the device safe. He was walking back to the rest of his crew and their ride, grinning and shouting to Iain that the first beer was on him when the hail of bullets almost cut him in half. Iain reached him and had just enough time for Jeff to whisper "tell Eleanor I'm sorry" before the light went out of his beautiful blue eyes. This job was personal, she wanted to make sure no-one else lost their man, son, brother, or father to these unconscionable men who sold armaments they'd usually stolen from military bases to fanatics.

Sa'id delivered her to a small, but clean, hotel in the old quarter. As she signed in, a woman selling ayran approached her, "salaam alaikum" she said, and smiled as she pressed a bottle into her hand. Eleanor didn't miss the drop of something into her pocket from the seller's other hand. "Alaikum salaam," replied Eleanor smiling and popping the bottle in her bag and handed the woman a dollar from her back pocket.

Her room was beautiful in old Moorish style. She flicked on the aircon unit, kicked off her shoes and flopped onto the very comfortable divan positioned by the balcony doors. The light breeze was very welcome.

She pulled out the note. It was her contact, Layla. It was good news; she reported having intel that 100% confirmed the property served as HQ for this cash-and-carry gun trade. Also, they had turned one of the men who worked there, and he'd revealed only this morning that there was a big 'pow-wow' tomorrow night between the Mr Bigs. The top men on both sides would be there.

The suppliers were coming in after dark to effect delivery of the biggest shipment yet. The shopping list they'd filled was long, lethal, and expensive. Layla's note said she'd meet her on the corner at 9 pm, and to call in a drone strike for half past ten. The note ended with the co-ordinates for the strike.

The hieroglyphics looked like a child's drawing, only her and Layla knew their code which she held momentarily over the lantern on the balcony table, then dropped it into the sink until it was ash and washed it away. She sent an email in another code to her handler in the UK.

Dressed in black stretch jeans and trainers and a reversible fushia-coloured shirt with black buttons, she left the hotel; the desk clerk didn't even look up. She hit the corner exactly at 9.00 pm. She was efficient in everything, including time keeping, was never late for anything. Her colleagues at the museum would describe her as cautious and precise, as well as helpful, shy, and friendly. They'd never have believed her capable of the other life she lived. That she was a top markswoman and had been asked by another government agency to join them as a sniper in their wet unit. But coldly taking a life like that was something she shied away from, it just wasn't her, no matter who the target was.

Layla stepped out of the shadows. "Hurry, the car is just down here." Moments later she climbed into a battered old Skoda.

Eleanor was certain that under the bonnet sat a pimped up powerful engine. As they pulled away, she removed her shirt, turned it inside out to complete her all-black outfit. Both had black balaclavas and gloves which allowed only their eyes to be seen, nobody could tell what colour their hair or skin was, and only Eleanor's eyes gave any suggestion of non-Arabic origins.

They pulled up in a small garage and Layla got out and pulled the doors closed behind them. As Eleanor got out Layla said, "it's just around the corner." They headed onto the roof, a small drone which had been delivered to Layla lay beside Eleanor's feet. Once assembled it would be able to allow them to hear and record what was going on in the building concerned and was the only access to it. They would position it near the corner, close to the main living room window, this also gave them an excellent eyeball on the street. It was Eleanor's job to get it all on tape as evidence of the 'righteous' kill.

By 10.00 pm, photos of men arriving in expensive 4x4s and elegant low-slung saloons that intimated bullet and blast-proofing had been added to its specifications. By 10.15 they had all they needed. Five of the world's most wanted ISIS leaders and five very prominent businessmen, including a retired US Marines Colonel, had said enough to sign their death warrants for treason and terrorism.

Eleanor made her final call from a throwaway mobile to an untraceable number, "blue boys are home" was all she said. Then she and Layla ran down the stairs and into the garage. Eleanor threw the doors open as Layla started the car. They were five miles away when the sky erupted in flashes of red, orange, and blue flames and plumes of white smoke, the strike was right on time. Eleanor cried for ages, she'd recognised one of the men in the video she'd shot, he'd been the local boss responsible for the attack on Jeff. It was done, she'd avenged her son's father. Rhodri would know when he was older, that the men responsible for the loss of his father was brought to justice.

She had a long and interesting lunch the following day with Sa'id about the proposal for the expedition, he said he'd let her know soon what their department's decision was. She was booked on a 7.00 pm flight, as she handed her keys in at the desk, the receptionist handed her a letter. As she waited for a taxi to take her to the airport, she sat and opened the envelope. Well, what do you know, the dig had been approved. However, she would not be the one to lead it, she'd delegate that, nothing would make her come back here.

Novella One: Poppy

Casualty Clearing Station: Merville, France, 1914

Len had been in the army since 1911; he joined up to give his family a better life than that of the alternative, mining. His unit was one of the first of the B.E.F units to arrive in France in Autumn 1914. Now, just months later, he and his pal, Bert, were all that were left of those seasoned soldiers who were first into the diabolic inferno of WW1 on the western front.

He listened to the nurses moving around the ward of the clearing station where two magnificent boys from the stretcher bearer teams had carried him to, in the early hours of last night.

They had cut most of his uniform from his filthy, mud-caked body, to clean and dress his wounds. Lying in the mud, blood and moonlight, he'd recognised the note of weary sadness that invaded the voice of the RAMC medic who was going to get him back to safety.

Sgt 26483 Leonard Baird was no fool, he knew his number was up.

"Nurse, when you have a minute, would you write to my wife for me please?" in a broad Scots accent. A voice replied, "Of course Sergeant Baird, I'll be with you in about five minutes, so get thinking on what you'll be wanting me to write."

"Will do nurse." Len relaxed back and pondered on it. He'd pressed a lovely scarlet flower last week in his bible, he'd planned to send it to Nancy in his next letter, he'd ask if his tunic was here. His bible lived in the breast pocket.

"Right Len, are you ready?"

"Is my tunic here nurse, I'd like my Bible if you wouldn't mind."

"Your pockets were emptied when you arrived as we couldn't save any of your uniform. All your belongings are here."

She reached under his bed and pulled out an old haversack, she drew his Bible out, "This'll be what you want" she said, pressing it into his left hand. He'd been blinded as well in the explosion that was to rob him of the right to watch his children grow and marry. Well, at

20

least there won't be another war after this one! The thought gave a modicum of comfort and made his death easier to bear, his children would live in a peaceful world.

For the next thirty minutes the nurse wrote all he wished to say, and he'd asked her to send to his wife the pressed bloom, "It's for my bonnie lass back home, my wife of eight years." The last three and half of which he'd spent in the army, seeing her and his two children only when leave allowed. He'd missed them terribly but wanted a better life for them. He was weary now and lay back and closed his eyes, he didn't open them again in this world.

Muiravonside, Stirlingshire

Agnes saw the telegram boy lean his bike against the hedge and begged the Lord's forgiveness for praying he'd turn to go next door. The Lord didn't pay her no mind, and Danny Ingles opened her gate, braced himself, wiped his nose then looked up to the house. He saw Agnes drop the curtain and move to the door. "It's okay Danny, it's not your fault lad. Off you go and thank you."

The tears ran down over the downy fluff on his sixteen-year-old cheeks. Nancy, as she was known in the village, slid down the back of the closed front door as she opened the telegram, her worst fears confirmed, "Died of wounds…"

The world lost its light for Nancy from that moment. Only Jessie, aged four and a half, and Davy, aged three, and the bairn she was carrying, the result of his last leave, would stop her from sliding into the darkness that beckoned.

They'd been blessed with a weekend alone in the week before he left for preparations for going to the front in the summer of 1914. She'd only realised she was in the family way again yesterday. Another bairn, another mouth to feed would arrive in the spring of 1915, around Len's birthday of April 13th, and sure enough Poppy, named for the flower Len had sent her from his deathbed, arrived hale and hearty at 1:30 a.m. on Saturday, 13 April. She was three years and seven months old when the war ended, and a legacy was born.

Davy rarely lost his temper or raised his voice, he was twenty-eight years old, married with a child, and so no fresh-faced youth.

He knew, as did everyone, that he'd be going off - like his father had done barely twenty-five years ago - but Poppy's talk of going too, was causing havoc in the family.

Poppy was a nurse and had - at age twenty-four - a perfect right to decide her own path. She'd joined the Queen Alexandra's Imperial Military Nursing Service five years ago. Now her senior officer had asked her if she'd be interested in joining her and some other nurses heading out to support our troops on the front lines.

Well, our Poppy had never been afraid of anything and had jumped at the opportunity to, "make a real difference" as she put it. Our mother was going ballistic. Our sister, Jessie, was also a nurse, but with no such ambitions to leave the hills and valleys of Stirlingshire. She was to be married next month and Poppy was intent on shipping out the following month. Mammy was in bits; she didn't care she was being left alone. Davy's wife, Fiona, was like a third daughter to her and she wouldn't be left to feel lonely.

It was the fear... Nancy could feel those icy fingers clutching at her already-broken heart again. She knew Davy would have to go, but her last bit of Len, no! she couldn't come to terms with that. And Davy was in the middle trying to broker peace between two of the strongest women he knew.

October 1939

Poppy had won, she always did. She shipped out on the last day of October, headed for who knows where.

Letters came thick and fast to Nancy for the first year that her baby was away. But as the U-boat packs built up their strength and ships were lost, so then did the mail become more erratic. She'd had a leave in early 1941 when she'd regaled them all with hilarious tales of jolly japes that had been had all over Europe's fields of blood. Her mother didn't miss the change in her daughter's eyes though.

In the autumn of 1942, Nancy received a letter from Poppy saying she had a leave coming and could she invite a friend, a highland soldier whose parents were dead and he'd no one to come home to. Nancy replied in the affirmative; Poppy had never spoken of any boy before, so she knew this one was special. He'd gotten permission from his superiors, and they got a special licence whilst on that wonderful leave. They married in Polmont's old parish chapel on a bright sunny Saturday in late autumn. Poppy Baird was now Mrs. Robertson, she didn't inform her superiors of her new status or name. She was still Sister Baird when she boarded ship heading for Italy in 1943.

Jimmy Robertson had stolen her heart when they'd met as he recovered from his injuries on her ward of the hospital. They both declared they knew from day one that they were meant for each other. They certainly made a handsome couple.

Nancy saw that same glow in her baby's eyes that had once shone in hers. She offered up a silent prayer that her youngest daughter would never know the pain of loss that she'd borne when Len had been killed in the last war, the one to end all wars.

During 1944 the starry-eyed couple had managed to grab two weekend passes whilst serving in the same area of Italy.

Now Poppy was devastated to be on a ship and heading home to Scotland. It was March 28, 1945. She'd been ordered home when somehow her superiors had learnt she was Mrs. Robertson. They'd allowed her a week to find Jimmy to say good-bye. She was furious, there was still so much suffering, there was still so much to be done. she felt like a deserter.

She arrived back to her mother's home on April 15, 1945. After the ship had docked in London she'd had to report to HQ to hand in her uniform and to sign her papers. They had not dishonourably discharged her, nor was her deceit recorded. That was her thanks for her years of dedicated service.

She was exhausted as the train pulled into the Waverley station in Edinburgh, twelve hours after leaving Kings Cross. Another three hours passed before she finally reached her mother's home. Fiona was standing in the door, there were tears in her eyes, "oh Fi, not Davy?" she softly asked. Fiona could only shake her head. Poppy flew into the house fearing for her mother, but Nancy Baird was sat at the kitchen table, staring at the telegram that lay unopened on the table before her, she turned a tearstained face to her daughter. Poppy looked from her mother's distraught face to the telegram, it was addressed to Mrs. James Robertson. Poppy fainted.

The next months passed in a blur of anger, grief, and sorrow.

The war ended in Europe that September, just months after Jimmy was killed.

The twins were born on New Year's Day 1946.

Leonard, forever after known as Leo, and Poppy Lee were both healthy and complete opposites. Poppy was the oldest by only four minutes, a quiet thoughtful and introverted child who was kindness itself. Leo was brash, loud, fearless and a joy to all who had the opportunity to meet this whirling dervish.

Both of Poppy's children went into a form of service, Poppy took her vows as a Sister-of-Mercy in Elgin; Leo went into the Peace Corps and was sent to Nyasaland in Africa.

September 23rd, 1964

Nancy lay in her bed. It was too much for her to get up today, Fiona would be popping in later. She reached for the little transistor radio that Davy had bought her. tt lit up. Sandie Shaw's "Always Something There to Remind Me" was playing. '

She loved the happy, bouncy melody. She did like a lot of the new music of today. Cliff Richard's "Twelfth of Never" was a favourite, as was Doris Day's "Move Over Darling," but Nancy's all-time favourite was Matt Monro's "Walk Away" and it was often heard on repeat on the portable record player that Poppy had given her last Christmas. She lay back on the pillows and dozed off wondering what Len would have made of all the changes that had occurred since they were starry-eyed teenagers.

Fiona found her later, a beatific smile on her face. She was buried next to the memorial cairn to her beloved Len, in the churchyard of Old Polmont Chapel where she and Len had been married in 1896.

January 1965

Leo opened the door to the offices in Chiradzulu. He was on a week-end pass; he'd been on duty for four straight months and he'd been glad of it. He'd needed to keep busy after returning from his trip home to see his grandmother buried. She'd been such a force in his life, they were always really close. He would miss her terribly, he always thought of her as his north star. Who would steer him true now?

He stepped into the office and lost himself forever. He drowned in that moment in the ice blue eyes of Greta Andersson, the Swedish administrator. It was a whirlwind romance. They met in January and by July they had visited her parents in Flen, garnering a reluctant blessing from her stunned father. They then returned to his home in Stirlingshire where they married on September 23, 1965, in the Old Polmont Chapel. He liked to imagine Nana Baird was there too; it saddened him that she wasn't.

She'd seen young Poppy take her vows ending her time as a novitiate, she was now the Serene Sister Agnes. Nancy had cried as she watched her gentle granddaughter prostrate herself at the altar of Greyfriars convent chapel. It was a fine sunny day as they'd walked towards the convent, she'd seen the ducks on the River Lossie. She recalled a time with Len before the war. It had been a day like this, by a river like this, that Poppy's mother had been conceived.

What would Len think of their first grandchild taking Holy Orders? That had been the last time she'd been out. The flu hit her on the following Tuesday and she passed six days later. Leo knew she'd have been enthralled with Greta and would have loved all the folklore of her Viking people.

May 1967

Catriona - Davy's daughter - had shocked her parents with her announcement that she was moving to the States. She'd been working in one of the big banks, and they had business offices in New York. Cat had apparently impressed the brass and they'd invited her to train as a computer programmer. Then they wanted her to head up their offices in the Big Apple. She'd accepted. Her dad was devastated.

Fiona was heard to say she'd always known that rural Stirlingshire would not be enough for her adventurous and curious daughter. Catriona waved her good-byes to the large collection of family from the gate at Inverness airport. She gazed one last time at the tear-stained faces and the snow-capped mountains that overlooked the runways, then ran up the steps into the plane and a new life.

1973

Cat did well for herself and didn't return to her native Scotland until 1973. She was booked on the last train leaving from Kings Cross at 10:00 p.m. on a fine July night. Her peace and hopes of garnering some much-needed sleep disappeared as what at first appeared to be a full regiment of kilt-clad warriors, marched in formation down the concourse.

Officers and sergeants yelled orders and instructions to groups, directing them onto coaches as they moved down the train. Four of these now noisy squaddies entered the closed carriage she had been hitherto, sharing with only an elderly lady. Though they were rowdy, they were well-bred, for they apologised to the elderly woman and smiled shyly at Catriona.

"No need to apologise boys," the crone spoke softly and smiled, "No doubt the lass will be glad of some company nearer her own age, eh lass?"

Cat laughed, "Well I had planned on a nap, I've been on the go since dawn. My flight was delayed in New York for two hours on the tarmac and it's been a tad frantic trying to get here in time for the last train out for Edinburgh."

"New York, you say, on yer holidays were you, lass?"

The question came from a dark haired, blue-eyed devil. She knew she was in trouble the second he smiled, and the dimples formed on his chin.

"No, I've been out there working."

"Oh, really. In the movie business, are you?" asked one of the other soldiers.

"Must be, she's a pin up for sure" winked the devil himself.

"Well, no. I'm a computer programmer for a bank. They offered me training when I worked in Stirling, then sent me to the States to the pioneering heart of computers. I have missed my home and family terribly so now I've transferred back. I want to be near them again."

"And where do you call home, lassie?" asked the old woman whom everyone now knew was Mrs Nellie Agnew of Edinburgh.

"I'm from Muiravonside, near Stirling. The family all live there, or in Polmont or Reddingmuirhead. Some of the wider family are miners. Our family is laughingly-called the 'black sheep branch' as we are all in some kind of service."

"So, what do the folk in your family do then?" asked Ian Muir, *aka the devil.*

"Well, Papa Baird, he was killed in the Great War in 1914. My dad served in the last one; his sister Poppy's husband died near Maserada sul Piave in Italy in 1945. I've a cousin, Leo, in the Peace Corps; his sister, Poppy, is a nun, working with the poorest of inner-city Glasgow. Another cousin, son to Dad's other sister,

Jessie, is serving in Ireland with the Argylls, and my brother, Ali, is a flying doctor in Australia. He's coming home next spring with his wife, Lorna."

"So is your name Poppy, too?" the devil asked.

"I do have it. I'm Catriona Poppy, but yes, all the girls descended from Len Baird carry it in his memory. Why do you ask?"

"I just noticed its recurrence. Is there a story behind that?"

Catriona spent the next hour telling Nancy and Len's story and the bones of her tree took flesh for her fellow travellers.

By the time they pulled into the Waverley Station, Ian and Cat had arranged to meet below the Scots Monument on Princes Street the following Saturday at mid-day. Both detrained with a smile on their faces and a new-found spring in their step. Love blossomed despite cancelled leave, train derailments and other everyday stuff that can interfere with the best laid plans.

They were married on September 17th, 1975, with full military honours. Captain Muir and his lady ran laughing under the arch of sabres from the church. Life was wonderful and full of plans and promise.

Once, when they were all sat around the dinner table with her parents, her mother - Fiona - had said, "Well, lassie, I'm impressed with your ambitions, the pair o' ye seem to know exactly what you want. "Just remember this though, God laughs as men plan."

"Pah," said Catriona laughing. "That's *men*... He's never encountered one of Len Baird's lassies eh Mum?" Everyone laughed, but Fiona felt a chill run up her back, and sent a silent prayer up for her daughter.

1975 - 1990

For the next ten years, Ian and Catriona were posted all over the world with the Black Watch. They had three children: Gordon Leonard was born in April, 1979, Ian David in August, 1982, then finally, Poppy arrived in late July, 1985. She was to be their only daughter and the only child of theirs born in Scotland. She was baptised Poppy Agnes Louise on September 23, the anniversary of the passing of her namesake. She was to say later in life that she was infused with Nana Baird's spirit that day. Her Papa, Davy, said she was the spit of his mother; the sepia photos spoke to the truth of his words.

Ian had done his twelve years' service and left the army in that year. That was how Poppy had been delivered in the bedroom once occupied by her great grandmother Nancy. Cat's labour onset had been sudden and swift, leaving no time for an ambulance to get her to hospital. The paramedics insisted though that both she and her daughter needed to go to hospital for the once-over. They were discharged next morning with clean bills of health.

Fiona and Davy found their daughter and her family a house near-by and were doting, loving, grandparents until both were killed in a car accident on the M9. They were returning from a rare weekend to Edinburgh to see a show in the Fringe, it was August 1990. They lie in the family plot beside Nancy and Len.

That August was a terrible month for the Baird clan. Jessie and Michael's son, Andrew, who was a lifer in the Argyll & Sutherland Highlanders, had been seriously wounded in Iraq and was being flown to the UK and on to Headley Court.

He'd lost both legs and his life hung in the balance. Jessie was at his side when her mother and father were buried; Michael went to the funeral in her stead. Everyone else from the issue of Nancy and Len stood at the grave in the beautiful churchyard of Old Polmont Chapel.

Andrew spent many months in Headley Court and many more still with physiotherapists and prosthetic makers.

He had a bionic hand now and the dog's whatsits of a wheelchair. He was finally allowed home twenty-two months after the bomb blast that ended his army career, and his chance for a family. He vowed he'd never marry. He was just forty-two.

1975 - 90 Muiravonside.

Davy's son, Alasdair, and his wife, Lorna, had enjoyed the past twenty years since returning from Australia to their close-knit family. It meant Christmases, birthdays, and to be fair, any excuse they could invent, had the large family gathering in one or other of their homes. Catriona and Alasdair's were the biggest two houses, so it was usually in one or other of these that the huge family barbecues were hosted.

All the younger ones got on famously and Uncle Andrew always appeared ten years younger after being at one of the clan gatherings. Lorna said she thought it was the loss of ever being a father that had hurt Andrew the most.

"I wish he could find someone," she'd said often, but she also knew his views and accepted it would never happen.

Poppy Agnes Louise was great pals with her cousin Poppy May, our quasi-Aussie in the pack. Alasdair was delighted when his daughter had begun training as a trauma nurse; she now worked in orthopaedics at the local infirmary. Lulu, as Poppy Louise preferred to be called, had been inspired by her cousin and friend and she, too, had trained as a trauma nurse. Both girls declaring that it's the first ninety minutes that decide the outcome of a devastating injury.

Alasdair was looking forward to the birthday bash. He was planning to celebrate his 50th birthday in some style.

Life was peaceful and full of love.

1999 Muiravonside.

"You can't be serious, Poppy!" he almost choked on his sense of *deja-vu*. "You can't go into a war zone, for heaven's sake, child. If it's excitement you're after, go away and do free running, bungee jumps, or potholing. I had to watch your great-great nana worry and fret whilst your namesake nursed all over France caring for the soldiers. I won't have your mother go through that."

Just then Lorna came from the kitchen, "Ali darling, I already know, and I say this with love. This isn't our decision to make. She's a grown woman now, at twenty-five she's old enough to choose her own path, just as Poppy did, and we did."

Alasdair looked from his wife to his daughter, the loves of his life.

"Oh God," was all he said as he walked out the front door calling Rebel to heel as he went.

"Don't worry, Love," said Fiona. "Your father's wee sister went off in 1939 and it almost drove him crazy, for unlike me, he and his mother knew the pain of the loss of a loved one in a war-torn land, so far from home. Just keep that in mind when next you speak to him."

"I will mum, but I won't be changing my mind."

2001

Both Poppy May and Lulu had signed up with the Queen Alexandra's Royal Army Nursing Corps and joined their unit in the November 2001.

Both girls passed through their basic training with flying colours. Poppy May was now only referred to as Red - due to her profusion of Titian red curls - as now Sister, aka, First Lieutenant Baird, and Lulu was her Second Lieutenant, staff nurse Louise Muir.

Akrotiri, Cyprus 2006

They were working in a hospital unit on the beautiful island of Cyprus when their deployment orders came through. They had served all over and were now respected and, in their eyes, wasted in these uneventful postings. That was changing.

They returned to Scotland and home for a week-long leave prior to deployment. Both knew the conversations that awaited them would be a rehash of those same ones had at Alasdair's 50th birthday bash. It was really only Alasdair who was so against their choices, and only because he was so afraid for his beautiful daughter and his niece. He also acknowledged now though, that as serving soldiers, neither had any real choice but to go or to buy themselves out of the army, and he knew they'd never do so. It just wasn't in the DNA. He and the family had to come to terms with the powerful legacy of Len's lassies.

They arrived in the evening of February 9th. The stars were the first thing the girls noticed as they alighted the helicopter that had brought them to Camp Bastion.

There were lights in the huge camp, but your eyes were drawn towards what they later learnt were the Takar Ghar mountains. Looking towards them from the helipad it was the stars that drew the eyes heavenward. In such huge numbers they peppered the dark blue sky and seemed to go on for ever. It reminded them both of home and the views of the Grampian mountains. Mount Vorlich was so beautiful, but so too were these glorious peaks.

They spent their first months very quietly, the odd ulcer to treat, and one lad whose appendix decided to burst without warning. In general, life was routine for that first eight weeks. Then there was trouble again in Sangin Province and a unit was being sent out on a medevac. Two soldiers were injured, and two Chinooks were preparing for take-off. Red and Lulu were up for their first taste of action, treating soldiers like this was why they'd joined up.

Alasdair and Lorna were woken by the telephone at 04:20 hrs on March 27. He knew that this wasn't good news. Lorna stood by his side when he picked up the phone; at the same moment he heard his mobile ring in the bedroom. That call had been from Ian and Catriona, Lulu was also a casualty.

The parents were to arrive at Selly Oak in Birmingham once both girls had been stabilised in the camp and flown home. The distraught parents were ready to go at a moment's notice, both cars were ready with full petrol tanks and cases packed and loaded.

Two days later, Catriona looked out of her kitchen window to the sight of two braided officers and a Padre setting course for her front door. In that moment she understood her grandmother's sorrow. Alasdair took the call from Ian telling them of Lulu's death and asked for forgiveness at being relieved his daughter was safe.

Lulu's body was repatriated through Wootton Bassett, the streets were thronged with residents from this small county town in Wiltshire, all doffing their hats and throwing flowers over the cars, including the one that brought their baby home.

It touched Ian and Catriona and gave them a modicum of comfort that at least their daughter's sacrifice was acknowledged. There were five cars, Lulu and four soldiers died in the rocket attack on their medevac

Chinooks. One soldier was in the same chopper as Poppy May; the strike on Lulu's ride had sent huge shards of metal into the side of the other bird, killing the soldier and seriously wounding Red. The Pilot and other crew in with Lulu, also died.

2471130 2nd Lieutenant Poppy Louise Baird was buried with full military honours in the family plot beside her grandparents and great-grandmother.

 Red was in Selly Oak for six months or so, she'd lost her left arm and had injuries to her torso and left thigh. She said later that it was her uncle Andrew who saved her. They spent many hours in the garden of her parents' home after her discharge. They'd saved her leg but she had a marked limp, she also now had a prosthetic arm; the rib cage wound had healed well. Her biggest loss was her friend and cousin, and her career as a nurse and a soldier. In her darkest moments she occasionally had thoughts that maybe Lulu had been the lucky one.

However, it was the drastic changes she'd seen in Andrew that got her through. He'd spent six weeks staying at a friend's place in Edgbaston so that he could be at Selly Oak every day. Coming onto her ward and spending every waking moment that he was permitted with her. It was during that time that she watched a minor miracle happen.

Love found Andrew in the form of staff nurse Katy Tierney; forty-nine years old. They clicked from the off. They were married in July of 2004 and Katy moved to Stirlingshire with Andrew on the day Poppy was discharged in the first week of September

Poppy May still struggles some days, but on the whole, she is doing ok. She trained for the 2006 winter Paralympics in Turin where she met Matthew Fairgrieve. Mat had also been injured in Afghanistan. He'd lost a leg and a hand in an IED blast, but when they looked at each other they saw only redemption in the eyes of their soulmate. They married in Polmont Chapel in 2008.

Poppy Louise Fairgrieve was born in 2010. She claims she wants to be a doctor, or a pilot. Her grandparents pray not.

Stirlingshire, from the author's personal collection

The Man Who Could See

In 1978, Daniel Swift was a reporter for the Gazetteer, the local rag in a small Northumberland town. He had been researching veterans' recollections from WW1 for a big piece planned by the paper for the 60th anniversary of the armistice. He'd finally tracked the last name on his list of the few still around, which, after an initial phone call with the son, brought him here at the home of Mr T and Mrs L Atkins, son and daughter-in-law of the veteran. Records showed Jock Atkins lived here with them.

He'd called ahead, and Lena, the daughter-in-law had welcomed him in. His son had told Daniel when they'd spoken that Jock was actually in France at the moment, for the anniversary of some battle or other. He'd gone with the Legion and Tom, his grandson.

Lena ushered Daniel in and after offering refreshments they'd settled at the kitchen table. There were medals, maps and photographs all spread out. Daniel began by checking he had the correct birth date for Jock, Lena confirmed it as July 1st, 1897. He then checked it was still on for him to talk to Jock on the phone. tomorrow? Time was set for 10.00 am sharp.

"Alright," said Daniel, "how about you just tell me what you know of his time between 1914-1918. I understand he was wounded, spending the rest of the war in hospitals. Is that correct?"

"Yes," replied Lena, "and I can tell you about his pals too, the ones he joined up with. They were called, Joe, Johnny, Albie, Alf, and Tommy."

Now, Albie was famous in these parts; his powers on the pitch were legendary. They say he could swerve and run like the wind. Ran rings round the back line of defence of any football team in the north, laughing as he feigned one way sending the opposition one way, whist he tore off in t'other.

Johnny, he was a quiet one. Dad said he was a gentle soul. He could pet any animal and could calm the most ferocious into allowing it to be handled even when they were injured or sick. She recounted the story Dad had told them more than once, how Johnny had his arm broken by a rider in the local hunt. Johnny was rescuing a cub, orphaned by the hunt. He'd stood in the path of a horse, the rider had kept on coming, certain this scrap of a lad would move, not realising Johnny was stood straddling the fox cub who would be trampled underfoot if he did. A brave soul, but not an adventurous bone in his body, he preferred a book to a bike any day.

She stopped and drank some water. Now, this lad I do believe I would have liked for myself, she winked and laughed.

Alf, the stable lad up at the big house on the hill, he'd been seen regular-like, up on the back of the wildest most fiery mount they'd let him ride. He'd tear across the top field as if the hounds of hell themselves were on his heels. And he'd be laughing like a loon as he took the five-bar gate soaring over in one fine sterling leap.

Dad always said, though, that Joe was the bravest of them all. The one who always jumped from the highest points first, who went into the haunted abandoned mine shaft before the rest of us. He also said Joe was the self-appointed protector of the pals, despite being the smallest of us. He took on Buster Smith after he'd thumped Johnny and stole his slingshot. Buster bested Joe, but not afore Joe broke his nose. Buster gave us all a wide berth after that.

Lastly, Tommy - dad's best pal. My husband and son, Jock's grandson, are both named after him. They'd been fast friends since before they were five years' old. On their first day at school, they left by the back door as their mothers left by the front. They spent the day in the woods. They were very shocked and disgusted to find they had to go again next day, this time into the firm hands of the teacher, Mr Temple. Dad said he scared them for a while, but by the year's end they'd declared him a top chap.

After all this information was taken down and photos taken of the memorabilia, it was getting late. "Okay," he'd said to Lena, "I can get the rest from your father-in-law in the morning. Are you sure I can't call him direct?"

"No, Daniel, I want to ensure Dad isn't upset, and that you actually get the opportunity to talk to him. He may have forgotten or not recognise the number and refuse your call. So, we shall see you in the morning, 10.00 am sharp."

There they were again sat at the kitchen table, Lena had told him pointedly, "I shall be on the extension line" she then dialled the number. It was picked up in Amiens. Moments later he was talking to the veteran.

"Ok then, so why are you calling me again? Oh yes, hello, you're the reporter chappie, yes?"

"Mr Atkins, hello, yes, I'm Daniel Swift from the Gazetteer, sorry to disturb you sir, I just wondered if I could have a few words about your trip. I was told to come this morning and Lena would ask if you could you spare me a few minutes?"

"Yes, alright, but it will have to be quick as the coach will be here soon."

"Right, Mr Atkins, just wanted to ask what you've seen, where you've been since your arrival yesterday, could you maybe give a vignette, if you will, of it all?"

"Ok, son, if you're sure that's what you want:"

The old man sat on the wall and began.

"Let's see. What can I tell you? Well, I saw Albie, racing across a field, football on his boot, the lovely long lob he sent flying forward just before the mortar shell cut him in half.

Then I saw Alfie up at High Woods. So smart in his cavalry kit, sword raised as his unit charged, out of the whole troop only a couple came back, he wasn't one of them. A machine gun cut them to pieces.

At high woods, one of them wrote to his mum to say how Joe had taken out a machine gun post all on his own. He'd gone tearing after it when he'd seen what had happened to a troop of cavalry, they'd been mown down on the brow of the hill at the edge of the wood. His unit said he'd fought like a lion and was on his way back to his men when the sniper shot him dead. Only Joe had realised it was Alfie's troop we were watching.

In the afternoon, up by Poperinghe, I saw gentle, peaceful Johnny, walking with the Padre, shaking, and crying, he had been so badly wounded, in his mind. They court martialled him; his mates had to shoot him. He should have been given a Blighty! He was no coward; he just didn't have the heart for it.

Then in the evening as we passed near Albert, I saw Tommy bending over me, telling me to hang on, and screaming for the medics to come help. He told our Sarge where to go when sarge said, "leave him lad, get to cover." Tommy was always such a loyal pal, we did everything together; school, dances, even joined up together, though really it was me who wanted into the fray. He just accepted that was what we'd do next.

I don't recall much after Sarge left us, I was told we were in no man's land for 41 hours, and Tommy never left me. Snipers kept trying to pick off the wounded during all the daylight there was. The stretcher bearers came for us at late on the second day, Tommy was lying over me, protecting me, he died as they carried us back to the lines. He'd taken four rounds for me. He was the last of my pals; it was spring, 1917.

So, that's what I've seen since I got here. Is that all now?."

"But Mr Atkins, I don't understand."

"No! I guess you couldn't, but since Passchendaele in November 1917, when I lost a leg and both eyes, those scenes are all I do see. Goodbye."

"Come on Tom," said Jock, "it's Albert today, a visit with my old mucker." Tom picked up the wreath as the coach pulled up beside them.

Photo by Matt Redding from Pixabay

An Airfield in England, 1917

Flying Officer James St John, dropped into the cockpit. He felt the muscles in his legs twitching to the same rhythm that caused the tremble in his hands. He was twenty, flying was all he'd ever wanted to do since witnessing the Bleriot's flying school display in 1912. Now, here he was deep in the tumult of the war to end all wars. He'd flown 28 missions; the RFCs life expectancy was now down to a terrifying 10-15 days.

He made the bumpy take off across the damaged flarepath of the camp, the spring sky a soft blue, spotted with puffs of white cumulus.

His body began to relax as it always did, when, before he had had a chance to react to what his eyes beheld, there, tearing towards him out of the early morning sun was a Fokker Dr1. The tracers were like a railway line of red dashes, a deadly umbilical cord between these adversaries, creating a deadly pattern in the Bristol F2's fuselage. Number 1 engine began to emit a filthy stream of black smoke.

James threw the plane over on the right then immediately into a radical climb; Zander - his number two - was on the Fokker's tail, it gave James a desperate chance to survive and get home.

The men and fire trucks raced towards the estimated point of touch down and they watched the obviously damaged plane heading into line for the landing. He'd watched, detached, as the men who make the difference between his life and death reacted to his very smoky approach. He was smiling. He was going to make it, he thought. In that same moment, his only engine died. He knew it was over, his luck had finally run out. The wing caught the tree and flipped the plane over, it was a burning funeral pyre when the fire trucks and ambulance reached the spot.

Another name on the reredos, another son of England's womb, returned to her earthy embrace.

The Few

High in the sky, into the blue,

up went the few,

holding each breath they drew,

and flew.

Then breathed again, or not

for some were lost, shot

down in flames, so hot

it flayed their skin from bone,

dying up there all alone. No,

had our mates, so,

we died as we lived, forever,

together,

we few, who flew,

who drew the line.

that none may cross,

whatever the loss.

We knew, we few,

who flew, we must do,

for you.

We could not fail, and so you, salute

the few, who flew,

Those Lions, who

were, flying crew.

An Old Friend

We were all that was left of the British Expeditionary Force, 6th Battalion Seaforth Highlanders pipe band. Three pipers, two snare drummers, and a tenor who doubled as our base drummer since Jocky caught it the previous month. We'd had a full complement when we left for France, we were all that had made it to the sea. It crossed my mind - in the coming days - that we may not have been the lucky ones.

From dawn 'til dusk for eight days the Luftwaffe planes dived, bombed, and strafed those beaches. It took them thirty minutes to return to their base, refuel, and return. We knew exactly how long we were going to live for, in increments of thirty minutes.

Death stalked us, hour upon hour of daylight. He became like an old pal, by some psychological trickery, our anxiety levels soared if Jerry didn't come on time, or worse if he skipped a raid.

Jamie McDonald and Rabbie Wilson, two of the drummers, were my pals and they'd been at my back all over the place. Being drummers, they marched behind me. We all joked that they had my back, and I kept a weathered eye out for frontal assaults. So far, we'd seen each other through some rough goes. Now here we were, looking at capture or death, trapped like rats in a hole, with what looked like the whole of the British army. We were filthy, cold, hungry, our uniforms in tatters and covered in our own urine and vomit, and worse in some cases. The manifestation of fear is neither pretty nor sterile, but filthy and humiliating.

It was June 3· We were squashed together like sardines in line on the mole, waiting to board a destroyer to take us back to Blighty. The planes were spotted on the horizon, everyone thinking, "Will it be our beach, or some other poor bugger's turn?"

This time the Stukas were heading our way, and us - with nowhere to go - packed tight like sitting ducks on the causeway. They came three abreast, their guns blazing. I saw the panic and the casualties as they made their first pass. Some men were jumping for the deck of the ship when Jerry came on his second run, some missed the deck and fell between the ship and the huge unforgiving wall of the harbour arm and died screaming as they were crushed between the two.

Most though were killed by the bomb that dropped directly on the deck among the stretchers holding the wounded. As the Stukas passed over us, I could see the face of the pilot, laughing, as he strafed the men on the beach and in the water, a cruel, cold light in his eyes. His face invades my dreams still, seventy-eight years later.

On his third pass, the tracers showed him heading straight at where we stood, I cowered, yet was relieved it was finally going to be my turn. I heard the rattle of the guns as they began their next burst, when I felt a hand push me and I tumbled off the great stone arm and hit the sea with a wallop. The water was rough and all I remember was a huge wave picking me up and dashing me into the great wall. I was knocked out and came to on the deck of a small sailing boat just as we pulled into Dover harbour.

I learnt from the Padre that none of my pals had made it, nor any of the rest of the band.

Now, here I am sprawled on the bed, lying in my own urine again, an old codger now, and death my old mucker, whom I knew as an idea only till those seven days from May 26th till June 3rd, 1940, that's when we became close chums. Now, I welcome him. I never knew who pushed me off the mole, a pal, God's will, a blast, but I've lived every single day for those men too. I am so looking forward to seeing them again.

Death's hands are cold as he closes his spectral fingers around my heart, and it beats out its last tattoo. Finally… going home to see old friends.

Nature's Law

I was trying to move the bed

when pain first shot through my head.

Then it felt like an elephant, pressed

with all his weight upon my chest.

My vision blurred,

and I thought I saw a face I knew from in the war.

And like the friends of old, he took my hand,

like any one of those that we left dying on the sand.

I've waited to see you for more than 70 years,

so, don't try to dissuade me with your pitiable tears.

I let you be, that day upon the sand.

You, out of all of your band.

It was no miracle, that you survived.

It wasn't a pal, that caused you to dive.

But even God must allow me my pay,

and now has come, your judgement day.

It was of course the face of death I saw,

come to collect me. It's nature's law.

Dublin Post Office

Novella Two: Canongate to Cannon Shell

Chapter One
Joe's Journey – The Beginning

On duty at Kilmainham Prison that day in 1916, was not where I'd expected to be when I joined up in the Town Hall in Portobello. I'd responded to two things. The first was Lord Kitchener's "Call to Arms" and the second, a white feather that Jeanie Fairgrieve handed me that Valentine's Dance at the Palais.

It was just before my seventeenth birthday, and she knew it. But her brother, two years my senior, had joined up in September 1915 and they'd received the dreaded telegram on February 1st the next year. He'd been killed in Palestine; he'd only just got there after having been in Gallipoli since last November when his basic training finished. He'd joined up after a local recruitment drive to replenish the 4th Royal Scots, the Leith Battalion. It had been decimated by both Gallipoli and the Quintinshill disaster in May 1915.

The train carrying half the battalion had crashed en route to Liverpool where they were to ship out to the

Dardanelles. Of the 498 men of all ranks entrained, 216 died and only 62 were left unscathed. Leith was then asked to offer up more of her sons to fill the deficit. The 62 and the rest of the now named 7th carried on, to fight in places like Canakale, Anzac Cove and Suvla Bay.

David Fairgrieve had been a talented footballer and a hero of mine. He'd been scouted at school by the Hibbs football team, one of two premier teams in Edinburgh. He had a glittering career ahead of him until he took the shilling. Within twenty weeks he'd been attested, trained, fought, and was gone, with not a grave to show for his almost twenty years. So, Jeannie's wee 'gift' didn't faze me as it might have, I understood her grief and anger. But it got me thinking, did other folk think me a coward?

A couple of pals from our street had gone with the 7th, and they were my age. So, I guessed I could, and should, go. I came from a family with a strong military heritage, our men had fought in battles such as Flodden, Killikrankie, and more recently in the Crimea at Balaklava.

"Well, I'd gone and done it," as my mother put it, but the hurt, fear, and anger in her voice made the words hold a different connotation than when I'd told my chum next door.

Five weeks into my training, my company Sergeant asked what I'd done in Civvy Street. I told him I'd fixed the new-fangled telephones for the toffs out at Morningside and the like, I'd live to rue the day I answered him. Within three days I'd been transferred out. That innocent statement was enough for the army to deem me useful elsewhere. The severe shortage of signallers, (due to the dangers their jobs entailed) decided my fate, and I was then attached to the 59th Div., Signals Company. This was a Midland Regiment.

Just my luck, stuck in a Sassenach regiment with a bunch of blokes who barely understood a word I said.

I'd no sooner found my feet when orders arrived, we were shipping out, off on Active Service. So, filled with bravado of how we'd soon be teaching 'Fritz' a lesson he'd not soon forget, and secretly worrying, afraid that we might buckle and let ourselves and our pals down, we readied for the off.

Nevertheless, there we were in temperatures around 70F on Thursday 27th April 1916, about to board a train for the front when a dispatch rider arrived at the station and our Captain came over after having been in attendance to the brass. "A change of plan, lads," he said, "We're not for the front, we're off to Ireland, so follow me and get settled aboard asap."

We were to be used to quell the rebellion by the "Fenian scum" in Dublin. Things couldn't get any worse for me!

Chapter Two
My Early Years

I was born in the Canongate part of the Royal Mile in Edinburgh, in early April 1898. Scottish, but of Irish extraction. My paternal grandmother, a Lynch from Co Clare, and my maternal grandfather was a Brady, and granny Brady was a Murphy, both originally from County Cork. My dad's father was a Scot whose line went back into the mists of time.

Our neighbours were all Irish and Scots Catholics. Next door, were my parent's closest friends, Auntie Mary and Uncle John to us. They were a bit older than my mum and dad, and their children were like big cousins or aunties and uncles, but Mary and John enjoyed the wee ones in our family and spoiled us a bit. Mary was old school, nothing went to waste. She kept anything that might fit the next bairn. She had boxes of clothes and shoes that her children and now grandchildren, had outgrown before they'd worn out. I'd been lucky as their son, Jimmy's boots were always in good condition when he outgrew them, so I inherited some good footwear. We all had attended the same local Catholic school, so we had inside info on the headmaster's foibles and fancies which allowed me and my sister, Catherine, to avoid some pitfalls and unpleasant interludes that my classmates endured.

By 1914 when war was declared. I was sixteen years old, and typical of all lads of that age was enamoured of the 'glories of war' that the auld fellas would regale us with when the ale had flowed a bit. So by the time that Jeannie had gied me the feather, I was more than eager to test my mettle in the fires of war. How little did I know!

Which brings me back to the point again, a catholic lad, of Scottish/Irish origins in an English Regiment, required to fire on my grandparents' people. I was horrified.

I went to see Captain Bulmer. I didn't like the man, for he was ever going on about how his family was one of the oldest, most prestigious, families of North Yorkshire. Well, so what, thought I? I can trace my line which includes Robert the Bruce, Malcolm Canmore, and in Ireland, Brian Boru, so three Royals trumps his boast, but I kept that titbit to myself. I needed to be returned to the Royal Scots, the oldest regiment of the line, and the 7th battalion was where I should be.

"The army couldn't expect me to fire on my own kind," I said to him when I'd been given an audience. The arrogant bastard laughed in my face when I pleaded to be transferred out.

"Why should good Englishmen have to do all the dirty work?"

He told me in no uncertain terms that I "would do my duty or pay the consequences." He delighted in informing me that in times of war, I would face the firing squad for cowardice. If he caught me less than eager to carry out orders, he'd ensure I was charged, and court marshalled for the 'bog Irish scum' that I obviously was. My fists balled and my temper rose in my throat, but my father always said revenge is a dish best served cold. So, I swallowed, saluted, and barked, "Yes, sir," about-faced and marched out.

He called after me, "I'll have my eye on you, Paddy."

Two days later we were rousted from our bunks at dawn and were told to report after breakfast in full kit. We were going to the Post Office in O'Connell St, the heart of the uprising. The word was the trouble was over. Apparently one of the leaders was injured and Patrick Pearce had sent a woman, Elizabeth O'Farrell, to offer Pearce's terms for surrender to Brigadier General William Lowe.

It was Saturday 29th of April. We were lined up covering the junction of Moore and Parnell Street. We watched in astonishment as both Commander-in-Chief Pearce and Brigadier General Lowe arrived, salutes and words were exchanged and Patrick Pearce handed Lowe his sword, Lowe accepted the sword and the surrender. Pearce's men, in formation behind him, laid down their weapons and were immediately arrested.

My eyes stung with unshed tears and my heart went out to Pearce. All men will fight for freedom from oppression, God knows my own country had had its share. My blood held some of the same DNA as these men, and rightly proud I was. Seeing these brave Irishmen defeated broke my heart.

We were to escort the transport taking the 'rebel' leaders who'd been ordered by Pearce to surrender to Kilmainham Jail. Some of the soldiers in the transports were brutal, even when they loaded the stretcher which, I was told, held James Connelly who was seriously injured and not expected to live. I'd later witness those same men sharing smokes with German POWs. Where did such hatred come from?

After seeing them received by another company into the cells, we were dismissed.

As we left Bulmer called me back, "You traitorous bastard. I saw the tears in your eyes for those rebel scum, what have you to say for yourself?"

"Nothing Sir," I snapped to attention.

"Nothing? You, miserable piece of shite. Well, be sure I'll have you before we're done."

"Yes sir, am I dismissed Sir?"

"Get out of my sight," he roared.

I saluted and left. Two lieutenants were with him, witness to the transaction. So, I kept my peace for now.

We, and two other companies, were rostered to guard the prisoners, Sean MacDiarmada, William and Patrick Pearce, Thomas McDonagh and James Connelly, though he was in fact held in the medical centre, so I didn't lay eyes on him until the 12 May.

Chapter Three
The Betrayal of Blood

Six men from B company were called out of general duties on the evening of May 2nd. We later learnt that they had been the firing squad for Patrick Pearce and Thomas McDonagh on the 3rd and Patrick's brother,

William, on the 4th. When C company had six lads go, we thought that would be the last of the poor souls held at Kilmainham, but we were wrong. Two more were executed on the 8th leaving, Sean MacDiarmada, an Antrim lad of 32 years, and James Connelly. Connelly was being held in the Castle, where a first aid station had been created in of one of the state apartments. Word had it he was close to death from wounds to the chest and leg.

Just before lights out, Major Bulmer, (a promotion, reward for his part in the capture of the rebels) stood in our barrack room door and bellowed, "If your name is called, collect your kit and step to the end of your bunk." Five names had been called when he deliberately turned to look at me directly, "Donoghue" he snapped, then smiled, it was an evil smirk, "Hurry up Paddy, I'm not waiting all night for your potato-loving arse ." He laughed and told us to follow him.

We were taken up to the top floor of the jail to a large room which contained six bunks, a table, and six chairs.

"Sergeant Smith, over to you, make sure they are briefed on tomorrow before dismissing them." He nodded to the other lads, "gentlemen" then as an afterthought said, laughing "and you, Donoghue." He left, whistling, as he marched down to get his dinner.

Smithy was a great Sergeant and he really wasn't comfortable with Bulmer's 'witticisms', but his was a difficult position.

"Okay lads, B & C company have had to do this, now it's our turn. You lot are to be the firing squad for tomorrow. There's but two left so it'll be over swiftly. You will be ready at 04:00 hrs and as the dawn breaks, the prisoners will be brought to the courtyard you've been shown. You will be at attention as they are brought out separately under guard. The men will be secured by their escort. Major Bulmer, the medic, and Father Aloysius will stand off to your right."

"The Major will give the order when all's ready. He'll call, Ready, Aim, Fire. You, if you have a Christian soul, will aim for the target over his heart. For if you miss or just wound him, the Major must administer the coup de gras, and he's slow about it, so show some mercy and give them a clean death. The medic will then examine the prisoner and pronounce death. The priest will accompany the body to the holding room where the body will be prepared for burial. Now get some rest lads and be ready when I come to get you. Goodnight."

Chapter Four
Execution and the Sound of Silence

I spent a wakeful night, my conscience screaming that I must not do this terrible thing, but if I refused, my life would be forfeit and it would save no-one. After what seemed like the longest night ever, the last two of the men referred to by the papers as 'The Irish Traitors', were being readied. I could face no breakfast and the tea and cigarettes were burning my stomach. We were fell in by Sergeant Smith and marched out.

Sean MacDiarmada was brought out first. They tied him to a post and hooded him, his body trembled but his head was held high, he didn't waver, a braver man I'd not seen. Ready, Aim, 'Oh God forgive me', Fire. The rifle kicked in my hand; his poor broken body slumped. Bulmer and the medic approached him, a single shot rang out and it was over. The escort put his body on the stretcher and took him back into the jail.

Next, I was horrified to see four guards carrying a stretcher. Bulmer barked out, "Donoghue, help them get that traitorous bastard onto the chair."

I put my rifle down and went over to the bearers, that's when I learned that James Connelly was no Irishman, but son to my Auntie Mary and Uncle John from the Canongate in Edinburgh. How in hell's name did he get here? I had no chance to find out. Christ what was I to do? A man who was like a big cousin to me, whose boots I'd worn as wee boy. It was surreal, like I was in a dream.

As we lifted him from the stretcher his eyes fluttered open, he took in quickly the place and time he was at. His wounds would kill him soon. Why did we have to do this to him?

He turned his face to me, the escort stepped away as I secured the last of the bindings.

"Is that you young Joe?" he whispered.

"Aye, Christ help me, Jimmy, it is."

He was suddenly animated, "Listen close to me, Joe. You can't change this and if you try, we'll both die. Aim true for my heart, don't let me down now lad, 'tis a kindness I'm asking."

"That'll do soldier," shouted Bulmer.

 Sergeant Smith came over and was about to place the hood on him. Jimmy looked up at him and smiled, but said softly, "Thank you, but NO."

"Fall in," said Bulmer. By Christ I was sorely tempted to shoot the callous evil man that he was. I took my place in the line, READY, AIM, Jimmy smiled and nodded to me, FIRE! And then there was silence.

Chapter Five
And Now to France and Flanders (*or so I thought*)

Within weeks I'd been transferred again. Mr. Bulmer suggested I be returned to my unit as he felt my Irish roots made me a possible security risk. That made me chuckle when I heard. The fact that it happened the day after we passed each other in the dark lower corridors of the prison, where he took my message as

I whistled Peadar Kearney's tune, the "Soldier's Song." That became the National Anthem of Eire.

He knew I was biding my time, but that I would not forget what he did, nor was I one of the terrified newbie lads. He was going to spend the war looking over his shoulder and he knew it.

Mind you, he wielded his power for all its worth until I got out of his clutches. Every filthy job. He made sure I was on the streets, or with the units assigned to search the homes of known associates of the fourteen rebel leaders who'd been executed.

That was the worst, the men in those units were cruel for the sake of it. Old women, dragged from their beds in the middle of the night, thrown into the streets in their night clothes. Having to wait, sometimes for hours barefoot in all weathers. Out in the street, whilst these, 'soldiers' wrecked their houses, smashing everything. Then using their rifle butts on the household, even the elderly and female.

I was called by Sergeant Smith one morning as I headed for the cook house, "Well lad, today's the day you're off, though it's not where you might be thinking, at least not right away."

"What's to do Sarge?"

"You leave on an RFC flight to Liverpool in an hour, you've a week's leave, then you will report to Glencorse barracks to join troops heading to the front, back to yon Kilties yer forever havering about."

"The Royal Scots, really sarge?"

"Aye Lad, now away and get your kit ready, oh and Private, be careful."

"Thanks, Sarge. You, too."

As the train pulled into the Waverley Station, I still hadn't figured out how I was going to avoid seeing Auntie Mary and Uncle John, and if I couldn't, what was I going to tell them? As it was, I needn't have worried so much. I walked up Cockburn Street into the Mile, heading down to the Canongate and home. I was just passing Old Tollbooth Wynd when a hand clapped me on the shoulder. It was Uncle John exiting the bakers with the morning rolls.

"Hello laddie, jings son you look fair done in, where have you come from, France, Belgium?"

"No, Uncle John, Liverpool and Ireland."

"Oh Joe, I'm thinking I'm not going to like this story you're having to tell me. I can see it all over your face. Best come in here so we can sit quiet, and you can tell me over a glass, whatever you tell me lad, I'm glad to see you home safe."

We went into the Cannon's Gait public house. "Two small beers and two chasers please."

I paid the barman and went to the table Uncle John had taken in the back corner away from the bar.

"Okay son, let's get this over with."

I took a pull of my beer and spilled the whole sorry affair up to the point just before the stretcher was carried into the yard in Kilmainham jail.

I sat in silence for a moment, "Joe, just get it out son, it can't hurt more than the loss of him."

I looked into the face of a man I'd known and loved since childhood; I was suddenly aware of the changes in him since I'd last seen him. His hair held more grey, his eyes no longer twinkled with the threat of mischief, and his shoulders drooped as if carrying a heavy weight.

"Come on Laddie."

I continued. I recounted the moment I came to realise that the 'Irish Rebel' James Connelly was Jimmy Connelly, Scotsman.

I told him everything. My feelings, thoughts, Jimmy's request, and finally I told him, "I killed him. My shot was the kill shot to the heart."

I began to tremble and the tears I'd held back in Ireland found release. Uncle John cried too, then he lifted his head and put his hand on my shoulder and said the very last thing I expected. "Joe, look at me son, thank you. Jimmy was fated to die that day, he was in pain and in the hands of his enemies, and the Lord in his wisdom sent him you. You stole the kill from them, and you released him from pain, with a loving heart. You fulfilled his last request. Thank you, lad, it means a lot to me, and it will to his mother as well. Now come on, lets raise a glass to him, then let's get you on home, sure you're a sight for sore eyes. Yer father and mother will be well pleased to see your face."

And so it was. Auntie Mary came through late on in the fore noon the following day, when she saw me, she pulled me to her, whispered, "thank God you're safe, and thank you Joe."

It was done. My parents were sad and shed tears when I'd confessed all that had occurred in Dublin. Their love and care lifted me from the darkness that had threatened to overwhelm me. Now I had to live for Jimmy and myself. Though part of me wanted to go AWOL and answer the call of the Dublin Brigade, but if I were to do that, I would dishonour the heritage of my Scottish blood and the regiment many a man in my line had served.

It was back to Glencorse Barracks I went, and by the end of May I was entrained for Liverpool once more, but Sergeant Smith was wrong, we weren't headed for France, but Egypt. This wasn't as bad as the Dardanelles we'd suspected, for the rumour mill reported we'd taken a pasting from the Turks. But due to the heavy losses, disease and terrain, Gallipoli was abandoned. I was going back to my pals, if there were any left. And shocking to me, I was promoted to Corporal.

Chapter Six
Egypt and Palestine – June 1916

The voyage out was a very pleasant experience as far as I was concerned. Papa Brady had often had me out in the Forth, fishing out of Musselburgh with him; it had given me sea legs. A majority of the lads aboard obviously did not - and suffered.

The NCO in charge of us, 'new lads' as he called us, was Sergeant Goldie. A bull of a man, intelligent, witty and an all-round good egg. He'd been a miner at the 'Lady Victoria' pit before joining up in 1915. He'd been out in Gallipoli previously, but a piece of shrapnel had determined an Medical Evacuation via hospital ship. Three months in hospital had him fixed up and had also earned him a promotion from Corporal to Sergeant and a mention in dispatches for actions at Suvla Bay. Now here he was off to Egypt and more action.

We stood on the deck the night before we were to get ashore in Cairo. He gave me some advice on how to stay out of trouble and how best not to get killed. I climbed into my hammock that night wondering what my initiation into war, proper, would be like and hoping I would prove up to the task.

Entering the port at Cairo was not as strange a sight to me as to some out on the decks that gloriously hot morning. Although Leith didn't have this heat, and as a result less of the pungent odours that were heavy on the wind. However, the bustle and noise were all too familiar. Leith, where my Papa Brady and others of my family lived, was my playground as a boy. The rush and tear of a port held no novelty. The men who inhabited this place however did, in their dirty white kaftan type dress and burnt almost black bearded faces were a wondrous and slightly intimidating sight.

Here, close to the Suez Canal, was such an important strategic position, was alive with British and allied troops; before me was a teeming Metropolis. The harbour, with its domed buildings sporting beautiful arched windows, overlooked the docks filled with all manner of craft. Tankers, Feluccas, troop ships and gun boats as well as a myriad of small sailing crafts of designs both strange and wonderful.

We were soon disembarked and loaded into the backs of army three tonners. The chaps collecting us caught us up on all the news. They'd been here since March.

We were part of the 52nd Division, tasked with the defence of the northern sector of the Suez Canal. A few weeks previously they'd had their first contact at Dueidar. The tale they recounted was straight from the story books, full of glory and derring do.

A combined force of German and Turkish troops numbering over one thousand had attacked the Royal Scots position three times, inflicting huge losses. The position was manned by barely fifty men of Pontius Pilate's Bodyguard. That was the proud nickname of the Royal Scots, as they are the oldest regiment of the line. This defensive victory was great for the morale of these soldiers so recently departed from the Dardanelles. Again, the thought crossed my mind, would I prove worth my salt in a similar situation?

We spent much of the rest of 1916 in the desert, dealing with assaults on the canal, acclimatising, oh and of course training and drilling, both in Cairo and Alexandria. We were deemed ready to take up our position with other companies of the regiment at Romani. We watched the desert change from winter to spring, whilst we guarded the Suez. Attacks of dysentery were proving deadlier than the Turks in reducing our numbers until August of 1917.

Chapter Seven
Bloodied and Promoted

Between the 4th and 9th of August 1917, I found out what I was made of at the battle of Romani.

The enemy had massed a combined force of German, Austrian, and Ottoman troops, against allied forces which contained the first of the Anzac troops to arrive in this theatre of war. We were under the overall command of Lieutenant - General Archie Murray - recently arrived from the western front. Our local commanders were Major-General Harry Chavel for the ANZACs and Major-General Herbert Lawrence controlling 52nd Division, and a brigade of 53rd Welsh

Division. We were joined latterly by 42nd East Lancs Division.

The ANZACs were being badly mauled and the 42nd were slow to move up to support and the 52nd weren't ordered up nearly soon enough and so a committed attack was not affected. For the most part the majority of the Ottoman force made their escape. We did some chasing and had some fierce fire fights, but on the 9th the Mounted Anzac troops attacked the Turks at Bir el Abd and were repulsed. The Turks then withdrew to El Arish. My first blood - and we had not been victorious - but I had done my duty well against a true enemy, I was pleased to have not let myself down.

The next sixteen months were on par for a soldier's life. Periods of extreme boredom, or unending drilling and bulling, or fast and furious actions. On those days your heart would beat so fast sometimes you'd be certain it was about to burst from your breast. The adrenalin was a great thing when in the thick of it, but the nerves jangled as it dissipated in the aftermath.

I had made another move up in the ranks - as happens in war - the positions are vacated more swiftly than in peace time and field promotions were rife due to the casualties we were sustaining. So, Sergeant Donoghue 5454 had to hobnob with the brass more than I liked, but the lads under my command were a grand lot and I was determined to do right by them.

This life was hard, but the fires of war were tempering a steely determined man out of a hot-headed eager boy.

I reflected. I had seen men blown to a bloody mist, shot in the face and hacked to pieces by the great Turkish Kilij, yet I had kept my head and the contents of my stomach. Friends had been made and lost and I had not faltered. I was satisfied, I could do my duty well and be proud of my soldiering. I was a man.

In March – April 1917 we were in actions at Gaza, where we had been taking a bit of a hiding. One afternoon I thought I spotted a glint of sun on metal on the tip of a wadi. Lieutenant-General Murray had arrived to meet with the local commanders, so we were on security piquet duty on a perimeter somewhat further out than usual from the camp.

I decided to take a shufti. I went in a wide arc coming up behind the wadi through the shrubbery on the left of where I thought I'd seen movement. Just as I was about to berate myself for being an old woman jumping at shadows, he lifted his head. A Turk, setting a sniper's rifle up on the crest, readying himself for a long-range shot.

My bullet took him in the temple, he knew nothing of the enemy who had spotted him nor felt death's breath on his neck. The shot brought men running and I was rewarded for my actions with a mention in dispatches. Archie Murray said I had saved his or one of the other officer's lives. He gave me two things to show his gratitude, a Sam Brown belt and pistol and a field promotion to Captain. I still have the belt and pistol, and it saved my life just before Christmas of 1917.

Between April and December, we moved from Egypt into Sinai and Palestine, fighting at Wadi el Hasi, Burqa and Junction Station, to name but a few of the battles where the blood of Scotland's sons was spilled so heavily.

Chapter Eight
Jaffa to Marseilles

In November, the New Zealand Mounted Rifle Brigade occupied the port of Jaffa, the 1st Light Horse Brigade's victory at Ayun Kara made this possible. However, the Turko German forces were too close, just 4.8km away on the far side of the Auju river, making the port still vulnerable to the enemy's guns, rendering it impossible for ships, or people, to use.

The enemy must be forced back. We, the 52nd Division, were tasked to carry out an assault on the river crossing. We blackened our faces and divested ourselves of anything that might jangle or catch the light of the moon and slithered into the cold water. It gets very cold in the desert at night.

Once on the far bank we set up a defensive position to protect the engineers who had to create a bridge of some sort to carry the rest of the division over. We were far enough back that the Turks were unaware and had not had the foresight to set sentries to watch their back. The whole force worked like dogs. The muddy riverside made it exhausting and dangerous. By dusk it was done.

When we came upon them, they were certainly up for the fight, and it was neither an easy, nor pleasant, task to break their resistance. These Turks are many things, but cowards they were not.

We didn't see the shallow riverbed in the murky pre-dawn light until we were on top of it. Six robed and bearded Turks had obviously been living and sleeping there. Our accidental discovery of them had caught them as they prayed. Guns not to hand there followed a desperate hand to hand, head-to-head, gouging, stabbing fight for life that went on for maybe three or four minutes, but felt like hours.

Finally, one of ours and all six of their men lay dead. As I disentangled myself from the robes and bodies, a movement out the corner of my eye alerted me to a man of about six foot moving fast toward me, an enemy. He launched himself at the same moment I drew my pistol. He landed heavily on top of me but died as he landed. Our bodies had muffled the shot and so General Allenby never knew of my point-blank kill shot.

I had not escaped unscathed however, his Kilij was embedded in my shoulder. I was removed to the hospital tent where I stayed for ten days. It was a clean wound and the shoulder joint had blocked the passage of the blade. It hurt, but no serious damage had been done.

Having taken the far side, the troops and supporting artillery crossed and forced the Turks to withdraw by 8 kilometres. This meant the port itself and communications between Jaffa and Jerusalem were now secure. Our river crossing is hailed now, as one of the most remarkable feats of the Palestine campaign. General Allenby's dispatch said something like, "reflects great credit on the 52nd that despite the added difficulties caused by the sodden ground and swollen river that by dawn the whole of the infantry had crossed. The enemy were taken by surprise and any and all resistance was overcome with the bayonet, not a shot was fired. It bears testimony to the discipline of this 52nd."

We were ordered back to Egypt after Jaffa; where we were in reserve and got some much-needed rest. We re-equipped, so much of our kit had either rotted or been stolen on the jaunt to Palestine and back.

How wonderful was that first bath! I never wanted to get out, and for hours the house boy brought great steaming buckets of hot water to top up my bath. Eventually though, space and time called an end to my wallow. Clean, and more than ready for a cold beer, I went down in my nice clean captain's uniform. I felt ready for anything - which was just as well - word on the wire was that we were to be sent to France in the not-too-distant future. Next day at officer's call, it was confirmed.

We sailed for Marseilles and arrived on 17th April 1918. The 52nd were concentrated near Abbeville until the 29th when we moved to Aire to continue war training. We moved up to the Vimy area in May and began our first tour of duty on the Western Front. It had taken me more than two years to get here.

I bumped into Sergeant Smith at the ambulance station: I'd gone to check on one of my men who had gone down with a serious return of dysentery. Smith was with a young lad with a shrapnel wound, he and a few of my old unit were there, it seemed we'd all had some adventures.

They told me that Mr. Bulmer was still with them. He'd been 'ill' and away on leave. Word had it that he'd been found hiding in an abandoned barn, miles behind the troops he was meant to be leading in an assault against the Bosche at Cambrai in Dec 1917. He had declared he had had a bang on the head from some debris from a shell explosion. Dazed and dizzy he'd stumbled in the barn and collapsed. He had a scrape on his helmet and so was sent back on the hospital ship to Blighty.

One lad in his unit declared he had seen him and he was all but incoherent, yet here he was back, just as arrogant, and twice as evil, I bet. However, he'd lost the Major's pip and was on an equal footing to me, and not in my regiment, so I didn't expect to have much to do with him, none at all if I had a say. I had decided he wasn't worth the effort of exacting revenge for James.

Chapter Nine
Albert to Arras

The verdant, peaceful country was changing as we moved down towards Albert. The nearer we got the more the scenery resembled my idea of some alien landscape. Not a building was left intact, no green fields, no trees, no birds, just wooden tracks, dead bloated animals and men lying in ditches and craters of slimy, oily water. Men moving this way and that, it must have looked to our Gods, like an anthill does to us.

We stayed at Vimy where apart from a wee skirmish or two, we had it quiet. On about 23rd July we were moved into reserve for eight days, then we were ordered down the line to just north of Arras. However, our first action was at Albert. The place had once been a quaint country town. Its Basilica, which once had been a glorious place of worship, complete with golden virgin and child statue on the top of the spire, her face looking down over Albert's cobbled streets and cosy homes. That same statue hung horizontally when we arrived, apparently, Jerry's artillery had hit it back in 1915, and it had hung like that until that August day when we felled it completely. There was a superstition that had grown regarding the virgin and babe, it was said that the war would only end when the virgin fell. It was to be a few months yet, but the war ended soon after.

I was enjoying being with some pals that had been sent to our regiment in the massive reorganisation of troops, and to fill the gaps in our depleted ranks. Gabriel Carmichael, and Billy Murphy, were cousins, Ian Massey and Jack Fleming had both been pals through boyhood.

Billy and I had been in the Leith junior pipe band as drummers together and had enjoyed the swagger of playing to a thronged Princes Street on one or two parades. Ian and I had been always off on our bikes or the bus, if we had any money, out into the hills, where we'd climb everything and anything just to get a better view. Wee Jack was a gregarious ball of fun and mischief and was very popular with the lassies. A flash of yon smile and those wee girls' hearts would be all o'a flutter. Ah it was grand to have them there. They were in different companies, so we had to try and find each other when we had a quiet spell, and that wasn't often.

Three days after the fight at Albert we were at Arras, and that was a trip into mud, blood, horror, and death.

We were in the line, to our left were our 5th Battalion and on our right the Midland lads with sergeant Smith and Captain Bulmer. I had told my men to relax and await orders. I knew we were going over the top come the dawn. We'd all done our last letters home in the days before Albert so there was no good reason to put them all on edge before it was necessary to do so.

I was in my dugout, writing up some reports when I spotted Bulmer heading my way, "What the hell is going on here man, your undisciplined rabble are lying about playing cards. Is this how you prepare your men for an attack?"

"Good evening Mr. Bulmer."

"That's Captain Bulmer to you," he growled.

I was going to enjoy the next few minutes…. I shouted for my batman, "Wilkins, get Captain Bulmer some tea please."

"Yes Sir, Captain Sir." Said Wilkins.

The look on Bulmer's face was priceless as the realisation hit him, he turned to leave, but as he ducked through the door he said, "You are still bog Irish trash, a lot can happen in the line," his sick evil face wore a parody of a smile, "I'm not done with you yet."

I laughed. The absurdity! Thousands of Germans were trying their damnedest to annihilate us all, and he was focused on me. I returned to my desk, I still had three letters to write to the families of lads I'd lost at Albert in a mortar attack. How do you say, there was nothing left to bury to grieving wives or parents?

Soon enough Wilkins arrived with a pot of strong tea and some bread and cheese.

"An hour till dawn sir" he said pushing the tea towards me. "Sir, permission to speak freely Sir?"

"Of course, John, what's to do lad?"

"Sir. Talk is Mr Bulmer is a nasty piece of work, but worse, he's a coward. His men talk and apparently, he's voicing a hatred of you that's worrying. Sir, just watch your back Sir, is all I'm saying."

"Wilkins, do not repeat that to anyone. It's bad for morale having this kind of stuff going around regarding an officer, but I thank you for your concern."

Checking my watch, I realised the moment was all but upon us, I went out strapping on my Sam Brown and carrying my helmet. I walked down the line of my lads, a smile to the veterans of this butchery, a handshake or bit of banter to give encouragement to those who had to go up and over the top for the first time.

Some had thrown up, others smoked, trying to tame the trembling, and some poor sods stood in puddles of their own urine. The waiting giving time for thought and imagining, it could turn the strongest stomach to an acidic pit of bile, which - like every fibre of the body it inhabited - wanted to launch itself free from this moment of agonising, paralysing fear.

Shrill high-pitched whistles all along the line and our piper striking up Scotland the Brave called every heart and boot to action. Men screamed, catapulted themselves onto the fire steps and ladders and over they went. Some stood rooted, but I had no time to do more than shout, with me lads, Alba gu Brath. We were on the Jerry line in the blink of an eye. Yet time enough for their guns to take so many that minutes before were tough, brawny men. Now, broken bits of flesh or twisted pain-riddled boys, crying with their last breath for their God or mother. No mercy was asked, and there was surely none on offer that day.

Our job was done. We made fire and got the billy can on the boil for tea. Callous? NO, just desensitised men in need of something normal to tether them to themselves and sanity.

Chapter Ten
Arras to Peace

I went back over the ground and into our trenches, I wanted to make sure that none of our lot were still there. I was checking along the line and as I entered my dugout, I'd thought to collect my greatcoat whilst there. I heard a whimpering sound, and there under my coat was Bulmer. A snivelling, quivering coward. I had no time to consider the situation as three men burst in, they had just been watching my back they said.

Bulmer tried to get up, to bluff a way out, but he saw it was useless and his eyes went feral. He pulled his Webley and it was his own sergeant Smith whose rifle butt knocked the gun from his hand.

Bulmer was screaming incoherently when they took him away. They told me later that he tried to charge them with assault on an officer. He was put under arrest by the MP's. I heard no more of him or the incident for ten days. I believed he'd escaped punishment again and been sent to hospital in England, that no other action would be taken. After all, he was an old money officer, not a field commissioned commoner like me.

We'd just come out of the front line for a rest after yet another action at Drocourt on the 2nd of September when I heard more of him. I was shocked to receive a visit from the Provost Marshall's office; I was required to give evidence in his court martial. Two days later I marched into the court, (a barn, that barely had a roof). Bulmer was clean shaven and smart and in control of himself. He glared at me with unconcealed hatred. I truly believe there was some real madness in him. My evidence given, I was dismissed and told to return to my unit. Forty-eight hours later I received a communique; I was to provide six men for the firing squad, he'd been found guilty of cowardice in the face of the enemy and conduct unbecoming.

It was September 12th, twenty-nine months to the day since I'd attended another firing squad, this time I had his task. The six men were his own, they'd volunteered, Sergeant Smith and five others who'd been witness to his cowardice or on the receiving end of his vicious character or pitiless acts.

He was escorted to the post, crying and struggling. There would be nothing noble in this soldier's death. They pinned the marker; the blindfold was on. I called, "Ready, aim, fire." The Padre stayed put as I went over, I bent low to check for a pulse or breath, he lived! I whispered in his ear, "This is for Jimmy Connelly," and fired my pistol. It was done, and it was from his own doing, not my revenge that had brought him to this.

Two weeks of marches and skirmishes brought us to the Canal du Nord. The 27th of September, we fought and marched on through the Hindenburg line, where we - the 4th company - were leading the battalion. Then on to Artois, and finally in November we were in Hershies, just northwest of Mons when, on the 11th the end of the war arrived.

Bloodied, tested, and with nothing left of the eager foolish youth set for glory and honour, we were done; well almost. We still lost a few in the days after the 11th, some men just don't want peace. It was not until April 1919, having been sent to Russia on further ops - this time against the Red Army - that we were to head finally for home. We marched through Leith in June. I learnt that Gabriel had died of wounds on October 25th in Merville and Billy Murphy was missing, presumed dead too. Ian Massey and Jack Fleming were alive but in hospital in Le Harve still.

Our Regiment had won five Victoria Crosses, the highest award for valour in the presence of an enemy. We lost 583 Officers and 10,630 other ranks. The guns were silent, we had fought, we thought, a war to end all wars.

Chapter Eleven
Joe's Jeannie

I was born Jean Fyfie Fairgrieve on a cold, blustery morning, February 21st, 1897 in a small village in Stirlingshire. My father, in fact every man in the village, was a miner, or a retired miner. After a terrible disaster in the local pit, my father, who'd helped in the rescue work and then in the retrieval of the bodies, (only twenty-six of sixty-six men made it out alive) decided we were going to live elsewhere. He wanted a cleaner, safer life for his family.

One of his sisters lived down nearer Edinburgh, where work was plentiful. Agricultural, industrial, and of course the flagship mine, The Lady Victoria, with its accommodation village built for the workers, was within reach for them to ensure employment.

All our worldly goods were piled onto the cart and we all sat on the cart, or the horse, or walked the nearly forty miles to Pencaitland. A house big enough for the family had been secured by our aunt and when we arrived tired and weary, we found a big pot of soup on the fire and scones and tattie scones in the press with some lovely home-made bread and a cured ham, we fell into our beds that night and slept the sleep of the dead.

Two years later found me living with a sister and a cousin in digs in Leith, near to where I began my working life, in Leith Infirmary.

At the outbreak of hostilities, I'd gotten a spot in the munition's factory nearby. Two of my brothers had gone to the local regiment when the call went up for volunteers to fill the ranks after Quintinshill and Gallipoli.

Like most young women I was loving this time in a way, we had more freedom than ever and down in Manchester, Emeline Pankhurst was doing her damnedest to secure the vote for women. I joined the local Women's Social and Political Union branch, and actively urged the men not in uniform to go and join up, handing out white feathers to any and all who looked old enough to be taking the shilling.

The sooner this war was done, the government had promised the vote providing the women quit their campaign during hostilities. The other side of the coin of course was the lists, posted daily. Thousands of casualties, all someone's son, father, brother, husband, fiancé.

I was home visiting my parents when young Liam Lynch arrived on his bike with the telegram. The first thing I noticed opening the door, was Liam was sobbing, "Ah Jeannie, am so sorry, he was my hero, I never missed a game he played in, I'm so, so, sorry." And this was how I learnt that my older brother was now just another name on the long list of thousands of the dead lying in some foreign field. In less than six months he'd joined, been trained, fought, and was gone. I was assaulted by a battery of confused emotions. Pride, anger, grief, disbelief, and such a sense of loss, and later, guilt. Guilt that I'd handed out white feathers to young men like my lovely brother, urging them to go and possibly die, just like my brother. I'd foisted this grief onto other families by my foolish, thoughtless act, it shamed me now.

The war dragged on, the lists got longer, their ages younger, grief was on the faces of her community like powder and paint on the tarts at the Palais on a Saturday night.

I spent my time, sewing, knitting, and working. If I wasn't at the factory, I was at the WVS packing up supplies to be sent for distribution to the oldest Regiment of the Line, Pontius Pilate's Bodyguard as they were affectionately called. Founded in 1633, and Lieth considered the now-named 7th Battalion, theirs. The Royal Scots!

Now in early 1918 hardly a family left living in the area had escaped the dreaded telegram. The streets showed scatterings of returned servicemen. With no government aid, many slept on the streets, afraid to return home to wives and families such were some of their wounds. Some slept on the streets, some with families, mostly they begged on the corners.

Desperate to feel a flicker of the once, virile manhood they'd left on Flanders fields midst the millions of shell casings and in those quagmire trenches, where the bodies of the dead were visible in the walls. The bars around the foot o'the walk were frequented by all, escaping, reminiscing, arguing, and bemoaning the way those who'd fought were treated upon their return. All grieving the loss of pals, a leg, their sight, their old future. And the women suffered and grieved the loss of their menfolk.

Husbands came home, less than the men that had gone, some total wrecks, their bodies and minds lost to their control. Others, whose physical injuries were so terrible that even the most loving mother would have winced at the sight of her once handsome son. Many were enraged that their womenfolk were living better than before the war, adding to their overwhelming sense of inadequacy. Wages in factories far surpassed the pittance paid in domestic service or in shops pre-1914. And the range of positions that had opened to them now was vastly different. They'd welded, built tanks, they'd built planes, flew planes, trains, and ambulances. They'd found a new level of independence, and confident, assertive women stood where once were timid house drudges.

I was in the Royal Scots Club, handing out tea and cakes to soldiers home on leave when looking up, I found myself face to face with Joe Donoghue.

"Hello Jeannie, you're looking well." I looked at the man, for gone was the boy I'd given the white feather to back in 1915. I could see in his eyes the aging that far outstripped his years. He'd seen so much, too much, my heart ached that I'd been at least in part responsible for him joining up underage.

"Hello Joe, how are you, you look so grown up now, your family must be chuffed to have you home. Are you back for good?"

"Well now, you've not changed a bit, still firing off the questions like a Gatling gun?" said Joe, laughing. She laughed too.

"Joe, I'm so sorry about the feather, it was so stupid. You weren't even old enough to go, I am so very, very, sorry, I was such a silly arrogant girl." Jeannie's face turned scarlet, and her head dropped.

Joe roared with laughter. In that moment she knew he'd exacted some measure of revenge in laughing at her. "Have dinner with me tonight and we'll call it quits, what do you say?"

We spent every possible moment of his weekend together, and when he was packing his bag ready to return to the front, she was shocked, but delighted when Joe announced, "when this is all over, I intend to marry you, Jeannie Fairgrieve."

I accompanied him to the Waverley to see him off and fought tears as I waved him and hundreds more off to hell. The general feeling is, it's almost over he'd said just as the train pulled out, but they'd been saying it won't last much longer every year since declaring that 'it will be over by Christmas' in 1914. They'd been wrong every year since.

I had plenty of friends and neighbours who would not be going down the aisle with their intended now, so many women who wore black arm bands and dark rings under their eyes. Women who were yet to see their twenty-fifth year, but looking at their eyes you'd have guessed them decades older. The worry, the praying, then the joy of letters and leave. Dealing with the rationing, the bombs from the Zeppelin attacks. They'd been dropping them in attempts to get the docks since 1916.

I'd was working in the munitions factory the night the bomb hit Sherriff's Brae. I'd been lucky, the digs in Cables Wynd were so nearby. In my building, we lost every window, and the chimney fell through the roof and ruined the top floor.

The nights were the worst, it was why I had volunteered for the night shift, it kept me focused and I could sleep in the day. I was earning more money than I'd ever have dreamt possible back in 1914, and everything worth spending it on was rationed. This meant I was building a very healthy nest egg. I dreamt of a wee house, Cockenzie or Portobello, near the water, but not in the grey, overcrowded, battered place that was Leith.

Joe's letters came thick and fast to begin with, but as the last big push went on, they dwindled further.

After the Armistice, Joe was sent to Russia and by spring 1919 when he eventually came home, his letters were few and far between and always cold and angry.

He talked about Ireland and how he had bad dreams about James Connelly, his experiences in Ireland when he first joined up. Also, two of his best pals were dead, and two badly injured in Le Havre Military Hospital still. He said he felt guilty, not a scratch to speak of and all those others, dead, or injured and changed forever.

I detected something else but would not get to know what it was for a long time; however, within the month I'd glimpse its evil face.

May 1919 and the papers are full of the Daill Eirann's letter to the head of the Paris Peace Conference, stating its case for independence. Joe's mood grew darker the more and more it became obvious that Westminster was reneging on its promise of freedom in return for fighting Hitler.

Thousands of true Irishmen had stepped up to the plate to help by the spilling of their blood to get freedom for Ireland. Now, those same men were called traitors and anger was bubbling to a head. Soon enough, the cap would blow.

De Valera's trip to the US was successful enough to get the US to petition the conference to allow Ireland to be heard, but nothing now could stop the war to be known as the Irish War, from ripping through Ireland and every house in the land had to decide their standpoint.

We had set the date for the wedding, August 25th, 1919, and managed to find a gorgeous ex-mining cottage in Seton Sands. A friend of Joe's had supplied two silk parachutes, which my sister and mother were transforming into the dream wedding dress. They had embroidered tiny forget-me-nots and bleeding hearts around the hem, symbols of fidelity and a deep and passionate love. I was so happy:

Our life together was waiting to begin as we stepped out the great wooden doors of St Patrick's church in the Cowgate. John and Mary Connelly came to the wedding and told Joe, that in true British style the medal offices had sent James's medals to them, (few know nowadays that James Connelly fought for the

British at the start of the war) John gave them to Joe, saying, "Jimmy would want you to have them, and in truth, there is precious little of him left, and this was all we could bear to part with." Joe's hand shook as he accepted the three; 1914 star, the War medal and the Victory medal and slipped them into his dress uniform trousers. He embraced the two old folk whom he thought of as family.

We both had accrued a fair-sized nest egg and after buying the house we had plenty for a romantic week's honeymoon in the Highlands.

We arrived at the Drovers Inn just as the sun began to set behind this ancient hostelry, the orange rays glinted on the waterfall that draped the 200 ft steep drop off the hill that had protected the Inn and the sheep penned at the back between the hill and the Inn over centuries.

Our room was furnished in period furniture including a draped four poster, I blushed as I caught Joe watching my face as I let the coming activities intrude on my thoughts. It had been a long day and I was tired, Joe suggested I have a long soak in the bath and he'd go down and have a drink while I relaxed. I spent ages in the claw footed roll top tub, in fact, I dropped off and was shocked to see it was now dark.

Hours later and obviously the worse for wear Joe stumbled into our room. I was devastated and angry, it was our wedding night, how could he be so selfish and stupid? I feigned sleep when he whispered, "Are you awake, Mo Chridhe?" the Gaelic for "my heart," here was the first hint that our union was not going to be the idyll I'd envisaged.

Joe acted as if nothing untoward had occurred when we woke next day, he again tried to initiate intimacy, but I was hurt, angry, and having none of it, at least until he'd apologised profusely. I pushed him away saying, "You owe me an explanation and an apology."

"Oh, Jeannie come on, I just got carried away, can a man not have a dram or two on his wedding day?" I was livid, "NO, not if he's left his new wife awaiting his return, it's just selfish and cruel!"

Even years later, neither could tell with any clarity the sequence of events from that moment until Joe walked out the door. Fragmented images showed flashes of a fist, the shock of impact, the pain, the flurry of blows and the raging rant that spewed forth from my new husband's mouth. The level of his rage terrified me, then all went black.

I came to with Joe cradling me in his arms as he rocked me like an infant, tears pouring from him and sobs racking his body. "Oh God, what have I done, what have I become, I am so, so, sorry my darling, forgive me, oh please forgive me?"

Gently he lifted me onto our wedding bed, that's when I saw his valise was packed. I was confused, I knew I'd unpacked it the previous night. He followed my gaze, it's for the best my sweet darling girl, I'm sorrier than I can ever tell you, I will send money, but I must go. I'm not fit for polite company, I've become some animal, and until I best this beast, I must leave. Goodbye, please try to not think too badly of me."

I really couldn't get my head round this, less than twenty-four ago I was dressing for my wedding. Now, still untouched, I'd been abandoned by the man I loved and not only had he left me, but he left me battered, the bruises would take weeks to fade.

I received the first letter eighteen months later, post marked Ireland, he'd needed to take Jimmy's place he said, to help his cause for Ireland's freedom, in some measure to make up for James's death and his part in it. He said he'd also needed to work past his feeling arising from the war and all he'd seen and done. Anger, despair, guilt.

He had gone from our honeymoon hotel to Edinburgh's Craiglochart Hospital where Doctor Rivers was having some astonishing results with shellshock victims, including Siegfried Sassoon and Wilfred Owen, sadly Owen didn't survive the war.

He said he'd spent eight months there before going to Ireland and joining the rebels.

I settled into a life of work and home building, I knew in my heart Joe was the one and felt sure he would do everything and anything to find his way back to me and would purge his soul of the demons that had taken residence during the war. I worked in Leith hospital again, now training to be a nurse. I had a postcard from Joe every four months or so.

118

Then, in 1921, on a warm sunny August evening, I was sitting in the garden studying for an upcoming exam when I heard the front door open and close, as I stood to go in the back door, expecting Mrs Campbell from next door, Joe appeared in the doorway. He was a tad heavier than last I'd seen him, but he looked so well. Tired maybe, but relaxed. The haunted look so many had worn, and still wore, had left his eyes. 'My Joe' was back, I was certain of it.

He pulled his cap off and slowly stepped towards me, my heart was in my mouth, and could hear its pounding in my ears, I'd only had his vague non-personal cards to go on as to his ongoing commitment. I opened my arms to him, he did not move into the embrace, but slowly went to his knees at my feet, "Jeannie, *Mo Chridhe*, can you ever forgive me, I am so sorry, I hadn't realised how much the war had hurt me and how much rage was locked inside me. I promise you, I've exorcised my demons, only sadness and grief and gratitude are left. I am so grateful to have the chance to live my life, and hopefully to share it with you. I will understand if you no longer wish to be my wife."

The face that looked up at me was an older, wiser version of 'My Joe', my heart ached for him. My other brother had shared some of the horrors of France and Belgium with me to help understand what his eyes and soul had seen and endured. The best and the worst of men are seen daily in war he'd said. I gathered Joe into my arms and knelt facing him. We held the embrace for long minutes each with tears flowing freely. Then, raising his chin and with gentle hands cupping his face said, "Joe, I love you, you are my husband, and if your word is still your bond, we shall have a long and loving life together. Now get up," and laughingly added, "then get me up."

Post Script

Every so often Joe would go off to Craiglockhart and talk for a while, he never again so much as raised his voice to his wife, and they were blessed with three children. The eldest, Gabriel, was killed in the war that followed less than thirty years later, he lies in Kohima, he served in the 4th battalion, Royal Scots, just like his father. They lived a long, and mostly happy, life. Their youngest son, Jack, married and had two wee girls and their daughter Alex had two boys and a girl, all of whom were loved and spoiled by their grandparents. One of the girls joined the Royal Scots and served until it was disbanded in 2005.

Joe died on October 25th, 1965; Jeannie, a month later. She relayed this story to me a week after Joe's funeral. She also gave me this, Joe's account, he'd written it at Craiglockhart. He told her once this was his first draft, and the only one he dared let anyone else, but Dr Rivers read. Such were his demons and the horrors he described.

Public Domain Photo from U.S. National Archives

The Explosion Rocked the Street.

Tilly had just left the Millennium Mill factory, her shift ending at six thirty p.m. She lived four streets away and had just taken her coat off and kissed her mother's cheek, about to put the kettle to boil, when the world she knew rocked on its axis, and was altered forever.

Windows exploded, doors blew in and the front of the two up to down terrace collapsed. As the dust blew around them, her mother began to scramble for the stairs, "Nora and Tommy are up there," she screamed in terror. But as they reached the place where the stairs used to be and looked up, there was no, 'up there'. As their ears recovered from the blast, other noises began to filter through, screams, Klaxons, men's voices calling out familiar names. That's when Tilly thought she smelt gas. "Come on Mam, if the gas main has fractured, there'll be more explosions, come on," she cried, pulling her mother's arm.

The warden came running up the street just as people began to clear the pile of rubble that had spread to the opposite side of the road's pavement. He obviously thought we'd been bombed as he yelled, "Come on, to the shelter ladies."

Tilly's mother, momentarily stunned by the images before her, now began to scream and returned to try to climb the pile of bricks and crumbled masonry that until moments ago, had been her home.

Mr Wilkins, the warden, grabbed her arms, "Elsie, listen to me now, if they are under there, they are passed our aid, and only God can comfort them, if by some miracle, they are not, then they will be either at the shelter or the hospital, either way, you, and Tilly need to be fit to deal with whichever it is, so come on."

As they entered the shelter, two voices yelled in chorus, "Mam!" It was Tommy and Nora, it turned out the wee monkeys had been in James's room, Tilly's older brother - killed at the Somme the previous year. Their mother had refused to accept he was dead as no body had been found, and had kept his room untouched, in readiness for his return.

The wee ones had been under his bed looking in what James used to call his Secrets Box, at the medals he'd been awarded that lay there. They held his tin now, their mother grabbed them and crushed them to her ample bosom and looking over their heads to Tilly she said, "James saved them.   I know they'll always remember him now, and how he saved their lives the night the explosion at the munitions factory rocked the street."

At the Setting of the Sun

The Pipes cried and the drum beat slow.
The call to war, by some berated,
Whilst others called for glory, hated.
But those of us who knew to fear,
Knew we'd lose those held sae dear.

And the pipes cried, and the drum beat slow...

Men fought, died and tried, to reason through,
The horror of what man can do!
They marched in the mud and the blood and field,
Singing songs, but their fates were sealed.

And the Pipes cried and the drum beat slow...

When the lists are posted, when at last you know,
That brother John and his pal Fred,
Will n'er be back, for they lie dead....
Let the Honours lie,
I want a reason, why they had to die.

And the Pipes cried as did I, and the drums beat slow
by the graves we know.

Where a little girl with cherry lips and golden hair,
Danced and sang her nursery rhymes.
Where an old man sat to read the names,
And his mind flew back in time.

And the Pipes cried, and the drums beat slow.

That he lives still, when they all died,
Is still his cloak of shame.

And the Pipes cried as did I, and the drums beats slow,
by the graves we know.

As he looks off in the distance,
He sees his friends of old,
He's tired now, as his family call from the gates,
But he's had enough, he won't go on,
He can finally join his mates.

And the Pipes cried, as did I and the drum beat slow,
by the graves we know,
And the sun went down on Tommy.

Private Gabriel Carmichael's Grave

Photo from the family collection

An Act of Kindness

Lawrence and George had both received their commissions on the same day. Both sons of soldiers, veterans of Mafeking, and Ladysmith, both were eager to test their mettle as officers. Though secretly, Lawrie was not as enthusiastic.

Since the first day of their friendship, aged five in the military school in South Africa, George had always been the leader and Lawrie the tactician, and so it was now.

Returning to England after the siege and eventual relief of Mafeking the boys had spent the years from twelve to eighteen at cadet school at Sandhurst. Excelling, each in their different ways both sailed through the officer training and had passed out with glowing colours.

Deployed in Canada having taken up posts as junior officers until 1905, thereafter their units and finally the regiment was disbanded in 1908. At this point Lawrie and Gorge were seconded to the 2nd battalion Argyll & Sutherland Highlanders, and here they were to be found in 1914 as seasoned officers being sent as part of the BEF to France in August of that year.

Battle-seasoned officers after Mons, Le Cateau and the battle of the Marne, they had watched as the original men of the unit were killed and replaced, time and time again. Marvelling at the fact that despite being in the first wave every time they went 'over the top' they were still alive. Joking in the black humour habit of the military about this, declared themselves invincible and charmed. Quietly, in the wee small hours of the night, both men acknowledged it was but a matter of time. The average life expectancy out here was six weeks, Sod's Law said it was inevitable.

A changing of troops in their section of the line on July 2nd, 1916, was an occurrence they were sure was due to the losses sustained the previous day, evidence of those statistics lay in front of their eyes in no-man's land. The cock feathers of our men mixed with those of the Royal Scots, and the green hackles of the 16th Irish could be seen, lying where they fell, in a failed attempt to overrun the Boche trenches. We had not yet been able to clear the dead.

Now here we were again on the fire step, 04:00 hrs on what promised to be another beautiful summer's day, and the birds were in full voice, a moment of sheer joy midst the madness.

Lawrie had walked down the line to George's section, they shared a smoke and a snifter, and each left the other with a firm shake of the hand and 'see you on the other side old man' neither really believing that either would make it past the next thirty minutes

Lawrie desperately tried to make some spit, but his mouth was dry, he'd never make a sound from this damned whistle at this rate he thought as he checked his watch for the millionth time.

Then, all the time was gone, and the whistle shocked him when its piercing song flew forth and was astonished still further to hear from his own lips, a primal yell, a true battle cry. He tore up the ladder, the same guttural screams following him over the top coming from the men he was leading, so many of them, to their deaths.

The charge collapsed in the face of the fierce fuselage from the machine gun position in front of them. The arc of fire was about 120 degrees, there was no cover, no difficulty, no hope for those advancing, the enemy couldn't miss.

Lawrie was amazed to hear his name above the din, he turned to his right as George raced his way.

They were thrown into a shell hole by the blast of a shrapnel shell. When Lawrie came to, his eyes opened to the sight of George, who lay an arm's length from him. His eyes were wild, Lawrie grabbed his field dressings and water bottle, George shook his head, "Lawrie, it's no use old boy." Lawrie knew it too, had from the first sight of his dearest and oldest friend. His midsection had taken a terrible hit and now his intestines were draped over his legs, the ground, and a comrade who lay dead beside him.

"Lawrie old man, I can't feel my fingers or arms, you'll need to help me with this one."

"What do you mean?" asked Lawrie, terrified that he already understood.

"Don't be an ass, I'm done for, in a minute or two the adrenaline shock will wear off and I'll be screaming for hours till I finally go in excruciating pain. I can't get my pistol, far less fire the damned thing. I am sorry my friend, but I must ask a last act of kindness from you."

It was as Lawrie feared. "You can't mean that. No, I'll carry you back."

George smiled, "you know you can't, that maxim gun has to be taken out, before it wipes us all out."

"I can't, please don't ask it, you are my dearest friend."

"I must, there's no-one else," spluttered George through a mouth full of blood.

Lawrie slid in behind George, so his friend could lean back onto him. He stuck the needle in and pushed the small amount of morphine into his friend, his brother. George looked up and smiled, a weak smile, but a smile none the less. He didn't see Lawrie slide his bayonet up behind them. Lawrie hugged his friend, and swiftly forced the newly sharpened point of his bayonet up in the way his father's sergeant had taught the two of them when they were boys back in the veldt of South Africa. To kill with a blade, swiftly and silently.

George's smile didn't have time to leave his face before he was just another on the lists posted of the 600,000 casualties of the last twenty-four hours on the Somme, France.

The Boy Stood on the Burning Deck.

My place aboard HMS Goliath, ship of Admiral Lord Nelson's fleet, allowed me the pain and privilege of witnessing a battle moment in history that would in the future be remembered in paintings, stories and poem. My images, my words, however, are still all within my mind, my heart and across my soul. Here is my tale.

I began my life as a mariner aged eleven, as a powder monkey aboard The Intrepid. I'd seen many a sight and been part of many a scrap before the events of August 1st in the year of Our Lord 1798. The Intrepid and I had been involved in the battles of Yorktown, and Chesapeake Bay in the war with those traitorous colonials; by this time, I was a man and a naval rating moving slowly up the ranks, and was now a quarter gunner, junior officer!

When I joined, I wanted desperately to serve with my father, however he vetoed this, saying his captain would be put in an awkward position if one of his officer's sons had turned out to be a failure as a sailor. The pressure to never let him down was terrible to bear at times but gave me the steel to stand when my instincts said run in my first battles. I tell you this dear reader, that it might give you insight into the mind of a lad of twelve summers, who served aboard a ship in Napoleon's fleet in the Battle of the Nile.

We had been searching the Mediterranean for Boney's fleet for about three weeks when we happened upon her a short distance from Alexandria in Egypt. Napoleon had seventeen ships in his fleet, Lord Nelson only fourteen, and one - the *Culloden* - foundered before the engagement in the shallows.

Captain Hood aboard the *Zealous* led seven ships down the outside of the French line. Captain Foley, captain of the *Goliath*, my ship, snaked through a narrow gap twixt the foremost French ship and the shoreline, this is where we lost the *Culloden*, but it showed Nelson's brilliance as a naval strategist, we had the Frogs caught in a perfect enfilade, close quarter cannon barrage soon caused the decimation of Boney's fleet.

Within but two bells, the glorious sunset was lost in the darkness of smoke and flames from the cannons and the burning French ships. It was first watch at four bells when finally, the *L'Orient* took to flames, caught in the melee of sinking burning ships. By eight bells, she was in Davey's locker, that's ten pm to you!

But it's not the mastery of Nelson's strategy, nor the stoic, diligent resolve of her Majesty's compliment aboard the fleet, or the incredible images of man-to-man conflict that are caught in my mind like the magic lantern shows back home. No, indelibly printed across my mind, my heart and my soul, is the image of courage, devotion to duty, and love of his father by a child of only twelve years, the son of Captain Casabianca, late of Napoleon Bonaparte's Flag ship, *L'Orient.*

After the battle, a French prisoner related the details that give flesh and context to the images I personally witnessed. The image of the boy standing midst the dead and mangled bodies of so many of his comrades, bracing himself on fallen rigging, seeing the flames grow ever closer. What crossed his mind seeing the last of the crew abandoning their battle stations and ultimately the ship, knowing his father - the captain - had issued no such order? He would not shame his father thus.

I learned from the prisoner, that Captain Casabianca had been mortally wounded below decks and was either unconscious or already dead, therefore unable to respond to the calls of his son, requesting orders or permission to leave his post. The French tar added that as he himself prepared to dive overboard he heard the boys last appeal to his captain, "Father must I stay?" as the sailor surfaced the magazine of the *L'Orient* exploded. Both the captain and his son were lost.

Amidst this carnage, all fell silent. The sight of a lad of such heroic stature called all the men to stand in wonder, and to bless his soul for such courage and duty. In the midst of fire and shot, he stared death in the face, yet he held his mettle and refused to flinch. The explosion gave him a swift and honourable end and sent him on a chariot of fire into the arms of the Lord.

Now, as an old salt, I hear the tale of the boy told in ports across the world, and always I'm asked, was it true? Aye, I answer, every word and young master Casabianca is remembered well, in painting and in poem. His father would have been proud to call him son, and after all, that was what held young master Casabianca at his post.

Rosemary for Remembrance

The flutter of letters landing on the carpet announced the arrival of the mail. Alan left his breakfast and went to pick them up. Shuffling through them, he paused at a bulky envelope. Squeezing it gently he tried to learn what it contained before tearing it open.

Inside was a piece of card to which was pinned a sprig of Rosemary. Written on the card was the phrase 'Rosemary for remembrance' and accompanying it was a picture postcard. He studied it, puzzling over the strange communication and wondering who had sent it. And why a sprig of rosemary together with a picture of a country scene, what could this mean? He could think no reason for them to be sent to him. He didn't recognise the scene and was puzzled by the sprig of rosemary.

He put the packet aside and opened a couple of bills — which he irritably chucked aside — before going through the rest of his mail. Withdrawing a page of small closely written writing, he sighed as he recognised his sister's hand. Another plea for money with an endless explanation why she needed it. This, too, was tossed to the side and he returned his attention to the rosemary and the postcard.

Slowly chewing his toast, Alan gazed meditatively at the message. It must mean something, but what? He picked up the postcard and turned it over to look at the number written on the back. It started with 07 so it was probably a mobile number. Well, it might provide an answer to the puzzle so, reaching for his phone he dialled the number.

There was no reply and he cancelled the call when it was routed to voicemail. Still thinking about the message, he thought back, trying to remember everything, if there was anything in his past that offered a clue. Of course, there had to be, but he had suffered amnesia after his accident and could still not remember anything about or before it, though some sparks broke through occasionally. He tried the number again and this time the call was answered by a pleasant, sounding woman's voice.

"Allo, have you seen it yet?" the voice was heavily accented, French, or Belgian; Flemish, he decided almost instantly. He'd spent many hours in the company of both nationalities during his student gap year, he'd volunteered with the Commonwealth War Graves Commission and had worked primarily on the Somme. He loved languages and was now contemplating his retirement as a translator for the UN.

"Yes, hello," said Alan, "Alan Beauchamp here, was it you who sent me the card which I received today? I must say it's got my curiosity piqued. What's this all about?"

"Ah, *Monsieur* Beauchamp, I wish to invite you to a birthday party. My *maman* is seventy-five in two weeks and she would very much like you to come. I do appreciate you are curious as to why the intrigue. My maman has told me only this, she wished to reach out to you before it is too late, and to tell you, that your father - and my *grand-maman* - knew each other in 1943.

The rest of this story is not mine to tell and *Maman* refuses to tell me more until the party. She will send travelling expenses if you require. However, she does insist I tell you, that it is in your interests to attend. We are in a village called Wissant, near Calais, in the Pas de Calais region of France. Will you consider her request, *Monsieur*?"

"This is most unusual, however, my father always spoke with affection of the people who helped him after he was shot down in a dogfight over the channel, I do believe he landed somewhere in that area, so yes madam, if I can arrange a short leave of absence from my employers, I will come. Please send the information I'll need. A name and address would be a good start. By the way," said Alan "what is your name?"

"Cecelia" she replied.

"Well, Cecilia, *au revoir* for now."

A fortnight later, Alan arrived at the address on the very edge of Wissant. He'd parked the car, had some lunch, and enjoyed a short amble round the main part of the village.

He'd stopped at the church, it was a stunningly, simple place, but it radiated a peace Alan had seldom experienced. It also had the most beautiful stations of the cross on the whitewashed walls. A divine place, he thought with a wry smile.

Now, here he was, about to solve the mystery of the rosemary. The house was a single-story building, much like the miners' cottages in Scotland. He pulled on the old-fashioned bell. After only a moment, it was opened by a woman of about forty, she had a warm welcoming smile, he responded in kind, "Cecilia, I presume?"

"*Oui*, I am she, come in Alan, my *maman* is very excited to meet you."

"I cannot imagine why, but I'm definitely interested to hear of my father from people who knew him as a young R.A.F. pilot officer."

Cecilia led Alan into a very comfortable salon, where he found an elegant - if aging - woman in a wheelchair. She smiled at him. "*Mon dieu!* But you are like your father!"

He was instantly aware that she reminded him of someone but had no time to consider who before she reached out her hands, and with tears beginning to fall, she said, "welcome, my brother."

Alan was stunned. She squeezed his hands and drew him into the chair beside her. "I know this is a shock for you, I have always known of *mon petite frère*, our father showed me photographs of you on his visits over the years after your *maman* passed."

Some three hours later, Alan was sitting on a fallen tree in the orchard behind their house. The revelations of the afternoon had knocked his world of its axis somewhat, but it was a wonderful thing to learn he had more family; Amalie, was certainly his sister. His father's time in hiding from the Bosche until the resistance arranged safe passage home, had been less tedious than Alan had imagined. He laughed aloud and raised his glass; the sprig of Rosemary was now pinned to his lapel. And in his pocket, a photo of a young man with Amalie's mother, Violette, taken in the doorway that he was sitting looking at. Life was full of surprises, *Non?*

The Poppy Field

Nermin sat perfectly still. She was hiding in the cupboard behind the long heavy curtain from her kitten. She wasn't meant to have a cat, nor to encourage any into their small sparse home.

Her father mended cars, but since the soldiers had come to her homeland, work was scarce and if she was caught feeding the animal, she'd be in trouble.

She'd found Aisha behind the wood pile, a tiny creature that looked like an orange at first sight, mewling and nuzzling a larger cat that was obviously dead.

They'd bonded instantly. At nine years old, Nermin knew that the cat would die without milk, so she would steal away a small amount of her own daily glass and by adding a splash of water, she'd kept the marmalade cat from death. The cat was bigger now and stronger, and she kept the rats and mice under control, and so fended for herself.

Nermin found her tiny companion captivating, the playful bundle of fur followed her everywhere.

Late one morning, the two friends were playing hide and seek - as was their habit - when Nermin took the risk. Her father had left early that morning, before sun up, and her mother had gone to fetch water, two miles away. She concluded that Aisha's trip over the threshold would never be known.

As Nermin sat so perfectly still she saw Aisha through the small gap in the curtains which kept the flies from their food store. The little furball made a dash for her hiding place and launched itself onto Nermin's lap. She'd barely stopped giggling when the door to her home flew open and she heard her father's voice. He was speaking to someone, and unusually, he spoke angrily.

She was just about ready to come out of her hiding place and take her punishment when she realised there were at least three other voices, none of whom she recognised. She stayed quiet and was terrified by what she then heard. These were bad men; these were the feared Taliban. The thing most feared by everyone in her village was that these men would come to their homes and demand help.

146

Suddenly there was a resounding crash and a howl of pain, she also understood the words hissed at her father, "You will do this, you will do as I say or you, your family, and all your village will be destroyed, do you understand?" There was another thudding sound and a grunt before she heard her father's voice, faintly say, "nem fielaan," (*nam fallah*), he'd said yes, she felt her first tear fall.

A minute or so passed then the door slammed as they left. She stayed hidden, Aisha nuzzling her neck as if offering comfort. She must have dozed off as the sun had moved from the left side of the house. Movement on the other side of the house had woken her, she then heard her father leave. She ran to the window in time to see her Baba, shoulders slumped, moving down the road towards the headman's home at the foot of the hill.

Nermin was very curious as to why had her father been crashing about in the kitchen and the woodstore, she was still searching when she heard her mother's voice calling Salaams to their neighbour, Eima Nasreen. She bolted out the back door as her mother came in the front, she headed to the poppy fields behind her home.

Two nights later she woke to the sound of her mother's voice, speaking in a tone she'd never heard from her mother's lips before. She was pleading with her father, her voice full of breaks and sobs, "Husband, I beg you, do not do this, if we yield to them today, we shall never be rid of them or their evil and violence. And if the soldiers come and find these things, they will take you and what then will become of your wife and daughter?"

"Quiet, woman! We have no choice." The door slammed as her father left.

She quickly and quietly climbed out of her bedroom window. She could see torches and a line of heads moving deep into the tall poppies. She tried to see more by climbing up onto the roof of her father's truck but there was almost no moon, and plenty of clouds. As she climbed back into her room, she heard her mother's voice whisper in the darkness, "Oh, child, what have you done?"

"Nothing." She sheepishly looked up into her mother's face, "I heard something outside, I just went to see what was there."

"Get into your bed, you, foolish, foolish, girl, you have seen nothing, heard nothing, and you will never speak of this night ever, do you hear me?"

"Nem fielaan ummi. (*nam fallah umi*). Yes, mother.

Days later, Nermin was playing outside; as her father came out, he ruffled her hair and said, "Nermin, you are not to go into the poppy fields anymore, do you hear my words daughter?"

"Yes father, I hear you, but why?"

"Why does not concern you, just obey your father and be a good daughter and stay out of there."

She watched as her father drove away, he had some work in the next village and said he'd return at sundown. As if on cue Aisha ran between her feet then raced off towards the back of the house. Nermin chased after her, it was how their games began every day. As they played, she wondered what was in the boxes the men had carried two nights ago, and that had so frightened her mother, and caused her father to speak harshly to them both.

Aisha scampered into the high foliage of the poppy field. Nermin thought about not following as her father has commanded, but she had to get her cat.

She was more than half way across when she heard what she recognised as the big armoured vehicles that the British soldiers drove. They were pointing directly at her but would not be able to see her as she was so much shorter than the poppies. She ran, but not back the way she'd come, but at a right angle to the army convoy.

The driver of the first Jackal spotted movement amongst the poppies, the tip off they'd received said the Taliban were active near this village and were forcing villagers into helping them. They'd also said the Taliban had stashed a large amount of weaponry and possibly IEDs in this field.

Nermin's mother saw the military pennants across the field, she hugged herself, it had been a difficult decision to call the camp of the foreign soldiers, but she had to stop the Taliban from making her home a base, and from making their village a target. She had to free her husband from this awful choice, this awful promise.

The explosion took her by complete surprise, and had not only made her jump, but had elicited an involuntary scream from her lips.

She watched and waited to see what would happen next. It wasn't what she'd hoped for, not what she expected, not anything at all like the scenarios she had envisaged.

The young cavalry officer emerged from his vehicle as it stopped on the road that ran between the fields by her door, in his arms he was carrying what at first, she thought was a bundle of rags. Then the realisation of what her eyes could see, but what her heart refused to acknowledge, became one primal response. A bestial howl rose from her soul and exploded from her lips.

He carried her Nermin, he stood in front of her, her beloved daughter's broken body limp in his arms. In her arms she cradled a small skinny orange bundle of fur. The tears that streaked the dust of the soldiers' face reached her consciousness, but she could not find a way back to reality to acknowledge his sorrow, as the darkness closed in around her, she recognised the bitter irony in this tragedy.

Photo by Angelika Graczyk from Pixabay

Summer's End

Jack opened his eyes to a bright blue sky, small white clouds scudding swiftly in and out of his eyeline. The grass felt cool beneath him, above, a nightingale soared and dived in true abandon. It was a day like this, he thought, that he and Poppy had first met. Both racing down the sand, impatient to reach the water at Portobello beach.

The donkeys were out, and the beach was packed. They'd instantly recognised in each other a kindred soul as they tore oblivious to all and sundry until they hit the shallow warm frill of the water's edge. Within minutes they were laughing like drains as only children can, not self-conscious in any way, just high on the business of having fun. By days end, they'd sworn an oath of friendship. It might have proved to be a day out of a life but sitting eating sugar pieces and swigging from a bottle of Iron Bru on a blanket her mam had laid out, they discovered they'd be starting at the same school come September, when the new term began.

Her father had been moved here with his work from Ullapool up in the highlands. Jack would be her first friend in her new home. They were inseparable after that glorious day in the Glasgow fortnight back in his ninth year.

Years passed in easy friendship. They climbed Arthur's Seat and Salisbury crags, explored the castle, played footie in the King's Park, went scrumping and scavenged 'treasures' off the beach all year round. Jack helped her to get the hang of his sister's bike and they'd set off early in the day and cycle out to places as far away as Cramond, and Ormiston.

Lying head-to --head in the tall grass eating bread and dripping or dipping rhubarb into a poke of sugar, there was always something in their saddlebag for their lunch. Life was idyllic and innocent.

It wasn't like having a girl as a pal, she was as fearless as any lad he knew, she'd dived right into the fray when some kids from Joppa had decided that him being a Catholic was reason enough to warrant a good hiding. There were five of them, and Jack was taking a pasting. The biggest lad had caught Jack a good one and down he'd dropped, when she suddenly appeared around the corner. Instantly grasping the situation, she'd screamed and jumped straight into the centre of the melee straddling Jack's foetal form. Her fists up in a southpaw stance in a fair parody of our hero Benny Lynch, the up-and-coming Boxing champion.

The lads all laughed at this wee firebrand, but it was forced laughter, the glint of fearless challenge in her eyes gave them pause and they withdrew. Jack always maintained that that was the moment he fell in love with her. He was fourteen, she was thirteen.

Something changed between them that day and only the depth of their friendship held them together for the year following his beating. The easy rapport was replaced by an awkward tension that neither could ignore.

The summer of Jack's fifteenth year he spent on the farm at his uncle's in Ormiston, Poppy went back up to Ullapool to visit her Nana and Papa. Both were miserable.

In September, as soon as Jack heard she was home, he went around to see her. They went for a walk, from the Figgy burn to Joppa, stopping to watch the seals on the rocks in the shallow water close to the prom. As the sun went down kissing the Bass Rock, Jack told her how he hated to be away from her, and that he loved her, he would be sixteen the following day.

Poppy laughed in delight; throwing her arms around his neck, she said, "At last, I thought you'd gone off me, I've loved you since you rescued me from the tree when we were scrumping and the farmer was going to catch us, the year before those Joppa thugs bushwhacked you." Their first kiss was tender, soft, innocent, they both declared it to have been 'pure magic'.

Jack told his father he was starting at the Corporation as a clerk but wanted another job too as he wanted to marry Poppy, and they didn't want to wait much past his eighteenth birthday. For the next year or so he worked hard. His dad had gotten him in with the Hibbs FC, helping the groundsman and selling programmes on match days and being a general dogsbody. He loved it when he and Poppy sat looking at their savings book as the tally steadily grew.

Working at Easter Road had its benefits for a fitbaw-mad lad like Jack too. He had pitch side seats when Celtic managed a draw in the final that September just before his seventeenth birthday, he could hardly speak from the shouting and singing for days after.

Life was good. Poppy had blossomed into a Celtic beauty, wavy dark brown hair, vivid blue eyes and clear fair skin, curves in all the right places, and a smile to light the darkest night. They set the date, October after his eighteenth birthday, her dad had given permission for it, all was in place for a perfect life.

But God laughs as man plans. His call up papers arrived in the January of 1916.

The noise of a barking dog brought Jack's thoughts back to the present, it must be the second, or maybe the third he thought, for he really couldn't be certain of the date. What he was certain of, was it was summer's end for him. He opened his eyes again, the nightingale had gone, out of the corner of his eye something bright red was swaying in the long grass, he smiled a last smile, it was a poppy. He closed his eyes.

His father broke the news to Poppy, he brought her her letters and photo, though they were dark stained and smudged now. She held them close as Jack's father through his own tears read the telegram then the letter from Jack's commanding officer. He'd only been gone since April; now he was never coming home.

Poppy remembered the morning of July 1st; she'd walked back along the prom after finishing her night shift. Watching dawn over the water was always a great way to relax, and it had been such a glorious sunrise. She'd recalled their first meeting it had been on a day such as that…

Little had she realised as she recalled their first hello, he'd sent his last farewell.

Christine's Farewell.

Her coat a makeshift pillow,
As she lay beneath the willow.
The weft and weave of the swallow's tails,
carving paths across the sky.
Dissecting cumulous on high

The woody smell of sodden leaf,
Invaded, interrupting on her grief.
Wild garlic too and no mistake.
This too distracted and diffused the pain,
She'd never hold him here again.

She'd believed his promise to return,
To make her his forever more,
Instead, he flew, to crash and burn,
To die and lie on distant shore.

His things went to his mother,
The place his life begun,
She has his medals, books and pipe.
But me.............. I have his son.

The Flight

All Soul's Day, November 1, 2007. The old man in the bed had been drifting in and out of consciousness for almost two days. He knew his time was up, he was dying. He feared death, afraid to let go. He was in no hurry to meet his maker.

It was his duty. Thousands of lives had been saved; the war had been shortened by two years, everyone said so. And in the beginning, he'd been able to live with his actions, because of all these statements, and because he was 'doing his duty, following orders'.

But, in the thousands of days since that fateful summer morning, other facts had emerged. The horrors that had been visited upon not only the generations living that day, but subsequent generations. The births of deformed and damaged infants, it was the gift that kept on giving. It had cost the lives of approximately 135,000 from the bombing run, but many thousands more would pay for the sins of the fathers.

He'd seen nothing on that day except cloud. Clouds as they arrived, the final small opening and the bomb aimers call, "Target below," and his disjointed voice, "Bombs away." There were no screaming engines. Nothing except the flightpath there, clouds and the flightpath home, the huge sea that declared, "You're done, time to go home."

"Little Boy," as they'd euphemistically called the ordinance, was loaded aboard his B-29 Superfortress, that took off heading north from Runway Able on Tinian Island, one of the North Mariana Islands. He flew north then rendezvoused with two other planes who were part of the mission. One to take data readings and the other to film the raid.

His plane was first to reach Iwo Jima, as soon as the three were there they set off together. Their next sight of land was at 07:45 hrs, Tinian time.

They were flying at a speed of 230 miles per hour as they crossed the enemy coastline. Approaching the target area, they made a sharp left turn and after an eleven-minute flight at that heading, they began their three-minute bombing run.

"Bombs away," a sharp right and eleven miles later they felt the first shock wave. Retracing their flight, they arrived back on Tinian Island. A round trip of about twelve hours.

Twelve hours that changed him and the world forever. His plane, named for his mother, Enola Gay. His target mission, Hiroshima, August 6th,1945. As he lay there, knowing he'd soon meet his maker, he wept; he had comforted himself in the same way the Nazi's had, "I was just following orders."

He knew another pilot would have had to do it, but he knew now he was responsible only for his own soul, his own conscience. He believed he'd failed God in this. He slipped away with a prayer for absolution on his lips.

Photo by Wikilimages from Pixabay

My Mountain
Sumatra

Teruo Ito woke to the slither of a snake making its way over his legs. It paid him no mind; Teruo reciprocated.

He was feeling very weak. He'd had dengue fever before but never like this. The constant pains and nausea that had combined with the usual dengue symptoms were draining the last of his physical and emotional resources. It had also lasted much longer than usual. He was without energy, even postponing the collection of fresh water until today; the canteens were all empty. Now he must find the strength to get to the waterfall to replenish his supply.

He was almost sixty-seven but looked older, his body – usually muscular but wiry and tanned – today looked more emaciated. He lived simply in his self-built house high in the forested side of Mount Patah, on this beautiful isle in the Indian Ocean. He wore traditional male sarong and batik shirt. He'd stolen the ones he wore today from a washing line in a village on his return route from the sea.

163

Every year he makes a pilgrimage to the sea. Every year for twenty-five years he goes to see if his message was ever received. Every year he prayed, every year he hoped, and every year he stoically returned and began marking off the next three hundred and sixty-five days.

He felt so weak today, it had been more than a month, he knew this was more than dengue fever, he'd kidded himself in the first weeks, he didn't want to face his most feared moment.

He collapsed by the pool's edge, the waterfall in full flow. The water was fresh and cool, he slid off the side, leaving his sarong and shirt on. He had slept so fitfully through fevered nights he knew his clothes were damp and smelled of a scent he didn't recognise as his. He removed them as he floated under the torrent as it met the pool and the foam and the rocks. He beat his shirt and sarong on these ancient volcanic rocks until he felt they were clean, and hoped it was enough to dispel the rank and acrid scent.

Teruo dragged himself out and up onto the sun-baked rocks and left the sun to dry the clothes now back on his body, and he slept.

Dr Yamamoto had been studying men like Teruo for almost twenty years and he truly believed he would have the opportunity to meet one on this trip. He was a lecturer in Tsukuba University in the Ibaraki Prefecture, Japan.

Yamamoto had won a research grant which would allow him to get a field trip in between two of the universities talks he was booked for on this upcoming tour. He was speaking at venues in Korea, Taiwan, Singapore, and Cambodia. His flight was booked out of Changi to Palembang, where a private helicopter would take him and his assistant to near the base of Mount Patah.

Over the past two years he had arranged with students at Bengkulu college to do some 'on the ground' investigative research in and around the villages of the densely forest covered mountain. In that time, he'd received many little oddities that were interesting, but three that were downright tantalising and hinted at the possibility that one of these men that so fascinated him, might just be found.

Teruo Ito knew it was time. Tomorrow he must decide to do one of two things: one would mean he would never again look upon the face of his new-born son, who he'd left behind those long years ago, the other would be to bring great dishonour and shame to his family. He'd read all the pamphlets, all the propaganda that had dropped like snow over Mount Fuji-San, but he'd believed none of it. Japan would never shame itself so. Surrender was unthinkable.

The student accompanying Doctor Yamamoto was intense and passionate, reminding the lecturer of himself in his younger years. The combination of stories told by his *jiji*, ('grandmother' to westerners) of the Bushido warriors, the Samurai. Of his father recounting his wartime experiences against the Chinese. All this fuelled his young mind with a hunger for knowledge and built for these men a great respect.

Something lost by so many due to the west's judgements. Borne from a lack of knowledge and understanding of the beautiful Bushido code of his people. The Bushido code of respect and discipline gives honour to a warrior who offers to sacrifice his life by doing his duty and fighting, even unto death if required. To surrender was taught to be the act of a man without integrity, a coward! All of this put Akiro Yamamoto on the path to this moment in time.

The helicopter landed and they deplaned swiftly.

Teruo Ito forced himself to rise. He pulled open the large metal tube, in another life it had been part of a parachute drop to a unit of American GIs, they were buried as if heroes in a beautifully kept graveyard on the other side of his mountain.

He dragged an old naval kitbag out and removed its contents. An hour later Gunso (sergeant) Teruo Ito was ready. His uniform clean, and heat-pressed between hot rocks and stored away twenty-four years ago when his radio died. His white scarf with the vibrant rising sun of home was round his neck, every bit of leather shone, and his pistol was clean and oiled. His great grandfather's Gunto was razer-sharp and ready for combat. Genso Ito was ready for his final action as one of his Emperor's Samurai.

Akiro and Kato - his student assistant - were losing hope, they'd climbed deep into the forestation that covered Mount Patah, south-west of Palembang. Kato was about thirty yards ahead when there appeared a gap in the treeline allowing sight of the stunning waterfall ahead. Doctor Yamamoto agreed with Kato that there may be signs around such a source of fresh water that may give credence to their hopes and beliefs.

They approached the glade where the water had created a stunning pool. Verdant foliage and glorious flowers encircled this place. It also had a tangible atmosphere, almost sacred.

They'd stopped in awe just before the end of the trees, observing the fall in all its glory when the sound of breaking sticks and rustling bushes disturbed them and the birds took flight in a startled cacophony of a variety of squawks. Then, in the moment before they moved in reaction to this, a man appeared from beside the rocks of the falls, a soldier of the Imperial Japanese Army, but he was tired and frail, and old. They stood quietly to watch him.

Teruo laid his mat on the rock facing the waterfall, he removed his sword and broke the blade over his thigh. He knelt, Tanto in hand.

Akiro and Kato watched in frozen fascination. Suddenly the spell was broken and Akiro caused Kato to jump in surprise. The voice from his teacher was of a tone unheard in the university lecture halls. He spoke an ancient variation of *Nihon*. (Japanese)

He called out to the man, Gunso: "What are you doing?"

"I am Akira Yamamoto, descendant of Saigo Takanaga, if you are truly Samurai, you know who he was, he is called the last true Samurai. I know what you plan, I know why you do so, but I ask you this as his representative. I ask for one more day of your life. Maybe once we have spoken, you will change your mind, maybe not, but if you don't, I can take letters to your family. Will you give Japan one more day?"

Teruo was in turmoil; he'd fought himself for many weeks before finding the courage for Seppuku, but this man's ancestors deserved respect, and so he rose, and led them to his mountain home, such as it was.

Doctor Yamamoto thanked all the Gods that might be listening for satellite telephones and the world wide web.

Throughout the long hot afternoon and evening Akiro and Teruo talked incessantly. Teruo was astonished at the powerful tool that was Akiro's iPad. He was shown Hirohito's surrender, and his funeral in 1989, images of Nagasaki and Hiroshima. Of Tokyo today and - thanks to Google Maps - Ganso Ito virtually walked up the familiar street to his own front door.

By late evening a deep and abiding bond was forged between the two men. Teruo told of his experiences on the island and his survival over the past long and lonely years.

After they'd all removed themselves to a place to rest, Akiro sent a long email to a friend at the army base near Teruo Ito's home in Ibaraki.

Next morning, Teruo called the two new friends into his cabin, he'd emptied tins of fruit and meat onto large green leaves, "I thought to use the last of the supplies," he smiled at them and indicated mats for them to sit. As they began to break their fast, Akiro received an email from his friend, Gensui-Rikugun-Taisho, Fumihiro Tanaka. Otherwise field marshal Tanaka, to Akiro he was his childhood friend, Hiro. He looked up from the screen and broke into a wide smile.

"My friend, do the names, Yui, Takahiro, Sakura and Haruki mean anything to you?" Teruo's eyes were wide and tear filled as he answered.

"They are my father and mother. Sakura is my wife. Haruki is my son, a son I left when he was but a few months old." He dug into his pocket and from a battered old wallet pulled a small photo of a gentle faced woman holding an infant, "these are Sakura and Haruki."

Suddenly the iPhone began to trill and vibrate, "Hello, yes, I am Akirosan, I am so very happy to speak to you. Did Hiro explain everything to you? Good, then wait one more moment."

"Teruo, do you know the sound of your wife's voice?"

"Oh yes, I have heard it in my dreams every single night since I left her beneath the cherry blossoms in our garden at home all those years ago, why do you ask such a question?"

Akiro placed the iPhone on the mat before his new friend, he tapped the screen twice and the screen lit up with the face of a woman with tears flowing in abundance but who wore a smile of such joy too, "Teruo, is that really you, I await you still to keep your promise to return to us, will you come home now?"

She then turned from the camera and spoke softly to someone out of shot, "Anata, there's someone here who has waited many years to hear the voice of his father."

A handsome younger man came into view, in hushed emotional tones the man Haruki said hello to his father for the very first time. Many tears and questions later the call was ended. Teruo stood, his hands together as if in prayer, he bent from the waist and thanked his new friend Akiro and said, "Please can I go home now?" tears coursing down his face, washing away the weary lines of despondency and loneliness.

He would give thanks to his ancestors and his Gods for Akiro and the doctor at the hospital in Singapore who operated and removed the gall stones that had so plagued him.

He lives with Sakura in the same house his father and grandfather had brought their brides home to; his son Haruki did so too. Ganso Ito lives for the pleasure of his family and the joy his two grandchildren bring. He spends his days in his office where his Tanto and medals are displayed on the walls. There he sits writing his autobiography, it is called "My Mountain."

Photo by Yuki Mao from Pixabay

The Stag

Willie Geddes lay along the flat outcrop behind some scrub bushes. In his mind's eye, he was two thirds of the way up Ben MacDui. The Laird always asked for Willie to get the stag for the tables at the Hogmanay ball. He'd bagged some of the most majestic beasts ever seen by any Gordon Laird, or any laird in Inverness-shire, if he did say so himself.

He didn't move as the rock ptarmigan hopped past him, nor when the elegant golden eagle swooped down and not a foot from his face, nabbed himself a plump mountain hare. The spider had a good try at forcing him to shift, as it explored his ear, but finally it decided it was bored and moved on and left him in peace. He closed his eyes momentarily. He could see the five pointer, as it slowly ascended towards the ever patient, waiting Willie Geddes, dressed in the colours of the Gordon red muted tartan of his employer. A new kilt was only ever ordered when a new man came to the estate, Willie's was over eight-year-old, the Laird Gordon of Badenoch was not a wasteful man and so he bought the eight yard heavy weight kilts, for he knew they'd turn up again on the sons of the men of the estate ten or twenty years from now.

The huge powerful stag was now less than one hundred yards away from Willie's hide. He savoured the moment, appreciating the fine animal in its natural environs; the stag could not be bested in its magnificence.

The shot echoed around the valley.

But it wasn't his valley, it wasn't his rifle, it wasn't his shot. He'd seen the flash. It erupted from a small plateau nearly two thousand yards away. And it had scattered rock and dust just three feet from his left hand. Training and experience had told, and held him still, even from a sudden and unexpected report, such as that one.

It had been five years since he'd left the Lairds employ. When he'd asked to speak to the Laird, he'd been a little apprehensive as he was not enlisting with the Gordons, but the Argyll and Sutherland Highlanders. As it was, I was but two years with them when they too were disbanded, and we became part of 5th Battalion The Royal Regiment of Scotland.

Two and a-bit years on, and here I am in Helmand Province, Afghanistan, I'm one of the top snipers in the regiment, and I'd almost met my match and my maker. A shot of two thousand yards is no mean feat, but the record is almost three thousand five hundred yards not held by Willie, I hasten to add.

Whether the swoop of the eagle or the movement as the hare struggled for his life, something had caused the man to spook, or had he seen something in his sight that just jarred, didn't fit.

Wille didn't know, but he doubted it to be the latter. Sergeant Geddes was too good to make a rookie error in his camouflaging, not even the eagle had veered away from his position. His long range rife, not regular army issue, but the desert tech HTI. 50 was his baby here. The army issue was accurate up to one thousand yards, Willie was accurate up to two thousand five hundred yards, so was his rifle.

Willie is tired, his hip hurts from the flint like rock wedged against him, he has lain there in his own urine for the last seventy-two hours, the pebble he's sucking isn't doing it for him either now, and, his water bottle is empty. Soon the heat of the afternoon sun will fade, and the cold will chill him to the bone.

Just then he sees the tiny tell-tale movement that says his opposite number has given up, he has decided the sniper he's been sent to find, has moved from the area, and he's not being careful enough.

Willie exhales gently and softly, like a caress, squeezes the trigger. In his mind's eye he sees the regal beast fall to the bracken covered valley floor. He knows logically it is a man he's killed, but he sleeps better if it's the annual stag for the Hogmanay ceilidh.

Image by markschlicht, from Pixabay

Songbird

The first time Rosa had let her voice free it had come unbidden, she'd just joined in with people from her neighbourhood in their rousing anthem. The elders of the neighbourhood smiled awkwardly at each other. They wanted to acknowledge the heavenly voice of the innocent child. It was what it meant that caused their discomfiture.

Rosa however was ignorant of the song's implications, she had no inkling of this place, this time, this song and what it would mean to her and her family, friends and neighbours. *"Deutschland Ueber Alles"* to Rosa was only their National Anthem.

The next time Rosa sang with the same level of emotion or commitment was as they travelled to their new home. Many of the families of her street were also moving to the country.

Whilst she loved her city, she now looked forward to the countryside and drawing the trees, plants, flowers and maybe even some wild animals. Though due to the shortage of money and food, she expected very few animals to be still running wild.

The place they were going to was near to where her parents had often taken them in summer. She and her siblings had loved the house they'd rented in Fürstenberg. She sang as they travelled. All the 'Old country' songs her Babushka had taught her. Babushka Lena had been born in Russia but moved here when she was a young bride. Lena had taught her grandchildren the ancient songs, and now Rosa sang "*Hava Nagila*," (Let us rejoice.)

The young and innocent laughed and clapped in time, the old wept, for themselves, for their children and for the grandchildren whom they loved as only a grandparent knows how.

The third time she raised her voice to the sky, she stood in the snow and wind as she watched her parents and both her little brothers and baby sister pass in the column of those being moved to bigger accommodation. She would miss them, but she had a job here in the kitchens and her mother said she must help. She raised her eyes to the sky and from a heart full of love sang, "*Yerushalayim Shel Zahav*," (Jerusalem of Gold) and other songs of love and loss. She knew little of this, she was not yet fourteen. Soon she would learn, and the words would hold a new power and meaning.

After dinner that day, a kindly woman who worked with her, told her something, something she found impossible to comprehend or believe until she looked at the faces of all the women she worked with. After that day, she sang every day. For those who were ill, for the weak, for the children. Now that she knew, she so wished she could have sung Kaddish for her family. But she sang it every day after, for all the families. The women called her, *der singvogel*, (the songbird)

The last time the 'Songbird' sang, she walked with her neighbour. Rosa was a shy girl until she opened her mouth to sing. Then she was invincible.

Many who watched her that day talked of how she walked with her head high, even as she passed under the gate with *Ravensbrück* written above. Even as she approached the large brick building with the huge chimney. Still her voice held true as she lifted her voice to *Yahweh*, Lord of the people of the Israelites. Everyone who heard it and lived, swear they never heard Kaddish sang with such a voice again. So full of the Lord's Love.

They also said that the guard, as he closed the heavy doors behind her, wept as he silenced the songbird forever.

Photo by Dariusz Staniszawksi from Pixabay

The Promise

Morag sat looking at the tree and the array of presents so beautifully wrapped, it all looked so perfect. Everything was ready: tree, gifts, food. Her sister and parents were visiting and her daughter, now four, was dancing excitedly around the room in her new Christmas dress and scarlet glittery shoes. Anyone looking in through the huge sash windows could be excused for believing they were witness to a perfect pre-Christmas evening within a happy loving home. And this time last year they'd have been on the money. She let her mind slip back to Christmas eve last year.

Jack was chasing Jessie around the sitting room. She was refusing to hand over the angel for the top of their tree. "But Daddy, she's a fairy not an angel" she'd squealed as he lunged for her again. He played at being the wicked wizard, the evil King and finally convinced her, singing songs as the charming Prince from her favourite Disney Princess film, to hand it over. He lifted her up onto his shoulders as she screeched with glee, then helped her set the angel atop the tree, which glistened and sparkled with baubles and tinsel in hues of gold and green and blood red.

It had taken all their resolve to insist on her bedtime being at a reasonable hour. For them, as much as for Jessie. It had been a magical day and evening in their first home.

They'd secured the purchase of this lovely double fronted Georgian house in late autumn, and it had taken the last of their savings to renovate, decorate and furnish this gorgeous home. They'd so looked forward to their first Christmas, so much so, Morag secretly worried it would be an anti-climax. It wasn't, it was just perfect, the icing on the cake was just as they'd turned off the lights to go to bed, they saw the first flurry of snow falling in the clear starry skies.

They woke that Christmas morning to a good six inches covering everything. It transformed their garden into a magical place. A mini snowman was built, complete with coal for eyes and a long carrot as his nose. Jessie had run into the vestibule and dragged Jack's squadron scarf out, saying it was perfect for Sidney, (God knows where the name came from). Jack had laughed as he tied it round Sid's neck saying to Jess as he saluted, "It makes him look very dashing darling." They'd gone into the kitchen then and enjoyed hot chocolate with marshmallows, it made her feel warm thinking of it.

Morag pulled herself from the past as Jessie barrelled past her and launched herself onto her Papa's knee, "Papa, why can't Daddy be here for Christmas?"

Oh, Lord she thought, it's finally here, I have to tell her, however, her mother said, "Jessie, has your Daddy ever broken a promise?" giving the child no time to answer, she continued, "No, well, he won't now, so stop mithering."

Jessie knew Jack was often away for long periods with RAF 3 squadron, and names like Afghanistan and Helmand meant nothing to his daughter. Jack's unit had been deployed in May. It was for a six-month tour, so he'd said!

The morning he'd left he'd said, "Come on love, I'll be home for Christmas, and don't get Jessie's present till I get home."

Well, here we are she thought, Christmas eve, and since the "Crashed, missing in action" telegram in late

October, there had only been the CO's wife and the Padre's visits pushing to keep her hope alive.

Having got Jessie into her new unicorn onesie pj's and settled her into bed, Morag had gone out into the garden. Sitting in the love seat Jack had bought her for their anniversary in April, she lifted her eyes to the stars and prayed, and sent out her message on the wind, "Jack, please, if you are alive, come home, keep your promise darling, we love you and need you."

As she whispered her plea and released it onto the wings of her prayers, the tears coursed unbidden down her cheeks. She felt her mother's hand on her shoulder as she lovingly kissed her daughter on the top of her head.

"Have faith darling, it's Christmas, a time for magical things."

"Oh Mum, I'm thirty not three, he's gone, I just need to face up to it." A sob escaped her as she pulled herself from her mother's loving touch.

"I'm going to bed, goodnight Mum," were her final words as she went back into the kitchen, where the veggies were prepped, the turkey was in the bottom of the AGA, slowly to cook overnight. The champagne and orange juice sat in the fridge chilling for their traditional Bucks Fizz in the morning, and Morag felt nothing but sad, empty, and not a little angry.

It was still dark when Morag awoke to the breathless excited voice of her little girl whispering," Mummy, Santa is putting lots of presents under the tree."

Believing her daughter had enjoyed a flight of fancy or a wonderful dream, she pulled Jessie in beside her whispering, "Hush quick, sweetie, children must be asleep when Father Christmas comes, or he doesn't leave any presents. Come on darling, cuddle down quick."

Within minutes, Morag heard her child's breathing fall into the rhythm of sleep, and not long after she joined Jessie in the arms of Orpheus.

She too enjoyed a flight of fancy or a wonderful dream. In her sleep, she heard Jack whisper in her ear, "I won't break my promise darling."

The waking reality would have broken Morag's heart had it not been for Jessie.

"Come on Mummy, hurry, Santa has been."

She took off like a rocket heading downstairs.

"Jessie, slow down you'll fall."

The words had barely left her lips when she heard a scream.

"Oh God, Jessie, Mummy's coming."

Morag flew along the landing and took the stairs three at a time, but as she reached the foot of the stairs her terror turned to confusion as simultaneously, she realised Jessie wasn't lying at the bottom of the stairs and she heard her daughter giggle.

Thank God, she thought.

"Jessie," the word only half out as she turned into the sitting room, where she too let out a scream. Her daughter was sitting on Santa's lap, his beard had been pulled down revealing his face... *Jack's* lovely face.

She finally let all the tears fall unrestrained, her mother and father now having heard both screams joined them and were also in a state of shock. Her mother resorted to the standard, "I'll make some strong, sweet tea, that'll settle the nerves."

They then all sat together over tea and listened as Jack told his story of rescue and repatriation. He'd asked to be the one to break the news to Morag in person that he was safe. He was home for Christmas, and he'd kept his promise.

"Merry Christmas" squealed Jessie, "this is the best Christmas ever." She opened the present that Jack handed her, and a tiny ball of grey fur unfurled into the cutest kitten ever, "This is Alberta," she announced.

"Where does she get these names?" Jack asked as they all laughed.

Photo by auenleben from Pixabay

A Last Farewell

My love is not withdrawn and given now to him.
Both are of themselves, existing alone entirely,
In different space and time.
The love we knew was, both tumultuous and divine.
I was yours as you were mine.

This man is kind, he makes me laugh, again I am a
woman to adore.
He doesn't make me love you less, but rather love him
more.
Whatever all this is, it makes what we shared no less,
My love for you was no less true, and I was always true
to you.

I do not take his hand, to punish you for leaving,
nor as a process, part of grieving.
But I live on, alive,
And so, alone.
Must I stay in a dark and loveless life,
Grieving you as a sad abandoned wife.

His arms are real, and they hold me near.

His voice is gentle and dissipates my fear.

But make no mistake, my dear, It is him,

and not some ruse to keep you here.

He is he, as you were you, and,

in loving him, I am not to you untrue.

He is here, his loving brings, Both joy and peace.

And in moving on I find release,

From guilt and loss and longing.

to find maybe, a new kind of belonging.

The Firefighter

Ali was weary. Ramadan was twice as difficult in this heat, it drained all your resources and energy, and he'd taken all the leave he could during this fasting time. Hence the slightly jaded version of himself was the man who answered the call that blistering June afternoon.

The voice was that of his station commander, apologising for interrupting his leave, but this was a code red emergency, all personal leave was cancelled, and it was all hands to the pump. He was at the Mayfair station house forty-five minutes later.

Entering the operations room, he noted all his colleagues from both blue and red watch were already assembled and from the buzz of voices, were speculating. They'd been given scant details, for that was all that was available.

A fire had broken out in a block of flats and a call from a resident warned that he believed some druggies had been cooking meth in one of the flats.

They had no idea at this point what the cause, they therefore added this info to the list of possibilities, including gas leaks, faulty wiring and terrorists.

The block was close to Charing Cross rail station and the road closures were bringing central London to a grinding halt.

They were reminded of their training then dismissed to go assist the two stations already there. Soho and Charing Cross engines were visible as they raced to join the fray. They'd reached the tower block in good time, a blues and twos call meant sirens and lights, it certainly got the juices flowing before they had eyes on the fire location.

They were given orders to begin on 15th floor and work down alternating floors with red watch. They hit the 15th teasing each other as to who needed to cut calories and who needed more gym time. Things turned real serious, real quick as they opened the door from the stairwell to the landing and met a wall of black smoke. They donned their masks and began checking each other's kit, as always. Pulling each other's visors and straps down was routine now, they were all close, like family, closer in some cases.

They each knew the drill for clearing and securing each floor be that residential or commercial properties, the process was the same. Teams of two, they broke off to the left and right of the stairs and then to each side of the landing. Each pair working to clear the units of the trapped or injured.

Ali worked with Jake, they were opposites, in looks, temperament and background. One, an immigrant Muslim from Ethiopia. He, his brother, and father were all that remained of his family. His mother and sisters had succumbed on the walk out of the camps of brutality and starvation in 1993.

Jake was Irish Catholic, from a family who'd come to London in the 60s, his father had begun a small building firm and been lucky as well as good at what he did and now the business was large, safe and prospering still in the firm hands of his eldest brother.

Jake though had only ever wanted to be a firefighter. He and Ali met on the first day of training and had become firm friends. They were both made up to be assigned to the same station. They now knew each other so well they could read each other's body language and often second guessed one another.

Today no conversation was required. Ali checked the doors, turned handles, and took axes to locked doors, Jake was always first in, no heroics, in training they'd found they worked that way best. They went through the small flats quickly and thoroughly, securing doors and windows as they left, also marking each door with a cross, a sign for anyone else that this area been cleared. They were aware during the process of their opposite numbers escorting an elderly couple to the stairs where another crew met and escorted them out. It seemed due to the time of day, many people were out at work, the tally of injured would hopefully be low or zero thought Ali.

They were just approaching the last unit when the door of the last flat on the opposite side burst open and two men, shaven heads and heavily tattooed came tearing into Jake and Ali in the dense smoke. They saw Jake first and he began telling them he'd show them to the stairs, he was calling it in on his radio when Ali removed his mask to offer some oxygen to the shorter of the two men who was coughing hard. As Ali tried to help him, the man looked at Ali's badge then, staring into Ali's face, snarled as he screamed, "Keep your bloody hands off me you dirty raghead, I hope you burn here, filthy Muslim scum."

Both men took off down the stairwell before either Ali or Jake could do anything to stop them. They called it in and returned to check the last home. They had to break the door in as it was locked but they could hear someone calling for help. Ali's fast retraction from the doorknob alerted Jake and he stepped to the other side of the door from Ali smashing the glass box he unhooked the hose and made ready.

Ali, with one mighty swing of his axe, shattered both lock and jamb, Jake's gloved hand tightly gripping the handle prevented the door from swinging open, avoiding flashback. The whoosh of heat and flames shot past them, then instantly retreated. They moved in unison; Jake shot in, hosing everything in front of them; he tried the first door. Ali moved past and tried the next door, each clearing and securing as they went. Quickly reaching the last room where they found a woman sobbing and cowering in the bath, in her arms an infant.

She'd soaked towels and had climbed into the bath securing the wet towels over them creating a tent, her actions may well have saved their lives. The firemen carried them out, Jake had the woman and Ali the little girl. He held his mask over the infant's face and was rewarded very quickly with screams and coughs. They then hurried to the stairs and called in that they were clear on 15 and were heading down with a woman and baby. Just as the commander was about to sign off, Ali asked had the two men made it down. "Negative" was the commanders reply.

As they worked their way down, they could see that some floors were burning fiercely. Ali called in to the commander and said Jake could bring the baby and woman, who was now walking, down the last three floors and he'd begin working his way down the other floors. Jake could join him soon. An attempt to find the men had to be made. The commander was reluctant to let a lone man go off on his own, but he also knew that time was running out.

Ali smiled as he got the go ahead. He started on the left-hand side. As he came out of the third home he'd found with doors open and items scattered everywhere, one of the two men with tattoos came from a flat just passed the stairwell. He had a bag and was stuffing things in his pockets. The thief saw Ali, sneering, he made a gun shape with his hands and pointed at Ali.

It happened so fast neither had time to do anything, the sudden boom then a rumble and the right side of the block seemed to go down, as if it had taken a knee to the sky.

Furniture and concrete and dust turned the area into something you saw in movies. The right-hand side of the 8th floor was now resting, leaning against the remnants of the left-hand side of the third floor. There followed the appearance of smaller fires and explosions, everything he'd been trained for since the 911 attacks in the US, rushed into his brain like a host of angry bees, all vying for his immediate attention.

Just then he heard a muffled groan from the far end where the man had been. Feeling his way along the wall towards the sound, he called out saying to shout out and to keep doing so. A very croaky voice said, "Here, I'm here, help me."

Ali repeated himself and soon had a fair idea where the guy was.

To reach him Ali would have to jump from the seemingly safe left-hand side to the right's pile of rubble.

He took the rope they carried and created a lasso of sorts and threw it with accuracy over a huge steel girder end, pulling it, the noose closed securing itself. Ali yanked it hard four or five times to check, all the time the voice was calling for him to hurry.

Fixing his axe into his belt he lifted the Halligan tool and the jaws of life he strapped to his belt, he grabbed the rope. Almost as an after-thought he called his commander and quickly explained where he was and that a man was trapped, signing off before he was ordered to wait for backup. The man's cries were less frequent and not as loud or strong. He took the rope, and jumped, landing on a piece of the lift shaft, he called to the man.

"Ok mate, I'm here, I'm gonna get you out, call again for me." The man replied, "I'm here, help me, please!"

Ali saw the fires licking the debris just below the man. He was under a pile of kitchen cabinets, wedged with the weight of a washing machine. Time was crucial for crush victims thought Ali as he pushed his axe head into the space below the pile.

He asked the man his name. "Wayne. Wayne Jones," he said.

Ali asked him if he could move his arms or legs, he said he could, that it was his chest and the weight robbing him of breath. Ali told him to be ready on three to scramble out, as he didn't know how long he could hold the lift, nor if in lifting would he de-stabilise anything.

"Ok, Wayne, ready?"

"Yeah, mate, hurry up."

Ali shoved the axe as far under the biggest piece of the rubble and lifted, it was agony on his arms and back, both screaming from the strain. The man scrambled as fast as he could and was almost behind Ali ready to get to the safer side of this mess, when another massive boom roared through the structure. Everything shifted.

Ali only just managed to latch his safety hook onto the rope and grab for the man beside him. They clung to each-other as rubble and dust rained down on them. As it began to clear and settle again, Ali heard in his headset, the commanders voice asking for a unit sit rep. He was relieved to hear his colleague's voices calling in. All the while waiting to hear Jakes voice.

He called his name and number out and heard his boss's reply, his boss instantly asked where he was. Ali gave as clear details as he could when suddenly he heard a voice saying, "Well stay there, donut, I'm coming to get you." It was Jake, he was ok. Ali smiled.

"Ok now Wayne, we are going to get off here and go home to fight another day."

Jake and two more of Blue Watch arrived in minutes and before long they were safely on their way out.

"Do you know where your friend is?" asked Jake.

"He went back to his flat, he wanted to get something, said it was really important and was worth a lot of money to a mate of ours."

Looking upwards as they came into the bright sunshine, the building was burning and there was nothing much above the seventh or eighth floor on the right, most of it was scattered all over where the grass square had been.

Jake was reading the paper in the ops room a couple of months later, he lifted his head, "hey Ali, listen to this, that guy you saved, him and his pal were members of the National Front, and his pal blew himself to kingdom come when he went back. They reckon it was ANFO (*ammonium nitrate + fuel oil*). Apparently, he stole it from his work at a quarry in Sussex. Him and his pal were to deliver it to some bigwig in their group. They were going to blow up a mosque.

The one you saved spilled his guts and has denounced his previous support for the N.F. He said to the reporter that he owes his life to a Muslim fireman.

"That's you, my friend. Hey, donut, you changed the world a little that day."

They both laughed. Ali thought, "Inshallah, God willing. One heart at a time, eh?"

Photo by David Mark from Pixabay

The following novella contains situations and themes which may be disturbing to some readers. "The Vacation Killer Stories" continue through to page 254.

Novella Three: The Vacation Killer Stories

Part One - The Dispenser of Death

She was single from choice: it suited her lifestyle. She kept her dark side well hidden. The staff at the infant school where she worked would have described her as a dedicated and compassionate teacher who loved the children and lived for her work.

Hah! That's all they knew. They would stand united in their defence of her, rolling their eyes at the very thought of any impropriety or criminal activity.

But they were so very wrong, Lena was a sadistic inventive serial killer. Every year she holidayed in a different country, she lived for those weeks off, being her true self.

She would seduce some young man or woman, sometimes an older man. They were always so very grateful and eager to spoil her, but the fierce passion of the young always excited her to a higher place and left her wanting. When she had had her fill of enchanting and teasing her victim, she would whisper a rendezvous time and place, then strike.

She was devious enough to always ensure it would seem an impossibility for her to have made it to the meeting point, an alibi was always there, and the destruction of her latest lover would be deemed accidental. They never put two and two together.

Her first had been a friend from school, her first sexual encounter. Still flush from their erotic, if inexperienced, tumble in the back of his car. He had foolishly and incessantly, teased her, she remembered nothing of what followed. When she came to herself again, he was dead, and she felt amazing. His decomposed body wasn't found for over ten years. She had been reborn that day, she was the dispenser of death.

She loved her life, and their deaths.

Part Two - The Highlander

Lena strolled lazily down the cobbled slope that was the Royal Mile, her long flowery skirt floating round her legs felt wonderful. The city was enjoying a rare heatwave. She almost felt pity for the soldiers preparing for tonight's tattoo.

It was a night when both the television cameras were filming the show and a firework display ended the pageant. She had been on a few occasions to this wonderful event, but tonight's performance was going to be unique.

She'd met Callum two days before on the famous Rose Street: pub after pub from one end of the road to the other. A rich hunting ground for someone with her proclivities. With the tattoo and the fringe in full swing, the city was a hub of multicultural visitors to the daily events.

She'd been sitting in the shade from the late afternoon sunshine, scanning the revellers and pedestrian traffic for someone of interest, when a deep highland accented voice asked,

" Can I buy you a drink, bonnie lass?"

Lena looked up into a truly handsome face that was both masculine and beautiful all at once. She caught her breath, interesting! Delighted, she agreed to another white wine. Hours later, having drank far more than the one she intended, this glorious highlander lay sprawled across her rental flats large bed, divested of his kilt and shirt, he was a spectacular specimen. Unusually he was intelligent, witty and a considerate if seemingly insatiable lover. She knew she needed to be careful, this man could have what it took to touch her heart and that would never do. She'd agreed to meet him again two days later.

So! here she was, off to Deacon Brodie's to meet him, they would enjoy each other only for tonight.

Callum greeted her eagerly, kissing her hard on her still swollen lips pulling her hips to his, even eight yards of wool couldn't hide his reaction to her slow smile, her perfume, and her caress of his cheek.

Some of his friends and their girlfriends joined the lovers. They laughed and drank, exchanging charged looks and secret strokes throughout the evening. As the night drew to a close, she whispered in his ear,

" I want to surprise you, meet me in an hour at my apartment, I need time to get ready for you."

And making a show, kissed him soundly and left him smiling and waving. She knew her beauty drew men's eyes; someone would recall her leaving alone.

Her apartment was above a shop on the West Bow, near the esplanade entrance. However, the apartment Callum had been to, was on Jeffrey St, just around the corner. It had been booked online under a nome de plume, paid via PayPal on a throwaway mobile from a hacked credit card account. An Arabic woman would have been seen coming and going in a burka which jived with the paperwork. Lena, the schoolteacher would have been seen briefly on the Bow. The flat on the Bow could be reached via a shortcut through the wynd from Jeffrey St. So, her comings and goings via the wynd would raise no eyebrows. Nor would the pretty teacher and the woman in the Burqa be connected. This was not relevant tonight, she'd devised a very elaborate ruse, she smiled at its audacity.

Callum arrived into the alleyway on time, maybe even a little early, dying with the anticipation, she giggled to herself He saw her in the close and grabbed for her. She whispered,

" I have a bucket list, will you help me fulfil it one of my wishes?"

By the time she'd explained in graphic detail her fantasy, Callum could scarcely hide his excitement, the kilt lends itself to free expression in such circumstances. She smiled and ran her thumbnail up the inside of his thigh, she felt rather than saw the twitch and jump of his kilt. She bade him wait whilst she donned her disguise.

There were at least fifty baton twirling cowgirl dancers here from the USA, she'd seen the adverts for the programme and had made herself an outfit like theirs. It was simple to wear under a baggy top and flowing skirt. It was only a decorated vest and shorts. The hat was the problem, but she'd created a very good felt version that would pass in the dark. Callum was part of the support unit with the Argyll Pipes and Drums. He had his security pass which Lena had taken from his pocket and copied the first night as he snoozed in a post-coital nap.

He laughed when he saw her emerge from the toilets at the foot of the esplanade, she shoved her fine light skirt into his sporran, then grabbed him to her and kissed him with a fierce passion he'd so far not encountered. But then he really didn't know ALL the

212

details of her fantasy, it was the words unsaid which was causing the increase in her excitement.

She screeched and laughing loudly, took his hand, and raced up behind the stands, flashing her pass where required. He was desperately trying to grab her, she let him pull her into a passionate kiss in full view of the sentry at the portcullis, breaking away and pulling her Stetson low over her face, she laughed and in a southern drawl cried,

"Dahlin' we will be truly chastised for our tardy timekeeping if we don't run," and with that took off pointing her pass at the guard as she flew through the entrance to the castle. The guard laughed and said to Callum,

"You've yer hands full there, laddie, if you can catch her that is."

Callum had had to slow to get his pass out from inside his doublet.

"She'll be worth it mate; she knocks me dead."

He finally caught up with her near the "Lone Piper's" spot on the battlements.

She was hot with excitement already, but her iron-will discipline made slowing things down easier than it would for you or I.

She sat in the shadow of the Royal palace that rose behind half-moon battery. The passage between the War Museum, the Palace and the half-moon battery battlements were like the black hole of Calcutta she thought, and weeks of surveillance showed it was never used during the performances. The Lone Piper would emerge from a door almost opposite his spotlighted position on the gun emplacement.

She pulled Callum into the shadows and the doorway to the museum, kissing him, her hands gripping the hair at the nape of his neck with a fierceness that electrified him, and his instant gasp and aggressive thrust of his hips all but sent her over the edge. She allowed him to seduce her, it was as satisfying for her as for him, for she was delirious with anticipation of the conclusion of their tryst. There was a moment when they both were taken to heavenly realms, she momentarily, he forever. Finally, it was over, she knew he hadn't felt her remove his *sgian dubh* from his sock, nor the razor-sharp blade slice his carotid artery until he was in death's embrace.

She quickly focused and dragged him round and propped him against the wall directly behind the mark that guided the Piper to ensure the spotlight hit him directly. Then ran pell-mell for the gates. The baton twirlers were just coming back in, she pushed against the guard saying,

"Back in a sec, dropped my baton!"

She slipped back out onto the esplanade hidden behind the giant Chinese lion dragon heading out for their performance. As she reached the first stand, she dashed off to the left under the stands and headed for the toilets again. Secreted behind a water cistern was a small bag, a change of clothes, white T and black jeans, and a mousey bobbed wig. She headed off to stand eight.

The girl from the seedy side of Leith who was eager to earn the huge amount Lena had offered her to go and watch the tattoo until just before the Lone Piper was due to play. Then all she had to do, was leave. Lena had met up with her just before she met Callum, checking the girl had worn the same T and jeans she herself now wore. The girl cried when Lena had handed her the envelope bulging with £20's. The girl had wished her luck with leaving her violent husband and disappeared into the night. Exactly as Lena was going to do at the end of the show. She took her seat just as the lights dimmed all over the castle and the stands where the audience sat in eager anticipation.

The steady hum of the drones began the sweet sound, followed swiftly by the chanter's poignant melody and the beautiful lament of "Sleep Dearie Sleep," filled the esplanade. It was an apt tribute to the fallen highlander thought Lena. As the strains of the pipes died, so did the spotlight. The piper saluted, and turning he found, as the lights flooded the arena and castle again, that he was face to face with a terrible sight, that of his comrade and friend, dead.

The first volley of fireworks brought gasps of awe and approval, when suddenly they were interrupted with terrible screams as those in the top level of the stands spotted the body of the kiltie and the frantic actions on the castle terrace.

Lena joined some American women as the stands emptied. She muttered sympathetically to one who was crying, and with her comforting support, all the woman, including Lena, left the esplanade. Lena left them and turned right and headed for the apartment to collect her bags.

Thirty minutes after leaving the castle it was as if she'd never existed. Her flight to Sweden took off two hours after Callum drew his last breath.

Another great holiday she mused over her inflight champagne.

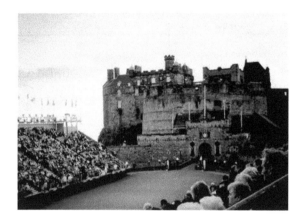

Part Three – The Italian Wedding

Lena had chosen the town of Rapallo on the Ligurian coast of Italy for this year's vacation.

There had been a point in the past twelve months, where she'd been so overwhelmed with the urge to kill, she'd almost asked for an early break. She had a will of iron and managed to resist. The months had passed, finally.

However, it had frightened her. Never, not even once in the twenty years since her first time had she hungered to kill before the designated time. She'd been just sixteen, still in school.

The thrill, the excitement, was like nothing on earth. She'd read later about serial killers, and seen plenty on television too, she'd been interested to hear how they speculated that it was the act of killing that was the ultimate sexual turn on.

This had never been true for her. She enjoyed a rich and varied sex life, and it never felt anything like the way she felt after a kill.

That was all about power and control, but it didn't mean she didn't enjoy sex with her victims, she chose them because she found them attractive.

Dumped at the door of a rural convent, abandoned by a vaguely remembered mother. Already broken, abused by her father and his friends or dealers. In a twisted way she thought the very act of abandonment was the one and only maternal action her mother ever performed, albeit unintentionally.

Lena thrived in the hands of the sisters of Charity. She enjoyed an excellent education and was often used as a poster child to promote the successes of the Catholic Church. Her quiet demeanour and perfectly beautiful face made her an obvious choice.

Since that first kill in her teens, she'd allowed herself one kill a year.

Once she could afford it, she travelled abroad; before then, she'd hitch-hiked the length and breadth of the UK and Europe, honing her skills annually. The kills were always random, the only connection was her attraction to them sexually.

She always found it amusing to think of them as a bonus, a holiday romance!

This year was the twentieth anniversary and warranted something special to mark the occasion. Nowadays a twenty-year anniversary is marked with platinum, but in older times it was china, and she was after all, an old-fashioned kind of girl!

Whilst on a long week-end trip about a year ago, she'd met Luciano, Luca, he was part of one of the oldest pottery families in Italy.

Descendant of one of Italy's masters, Giorgio Andreoli. He was an Umbrian from Gubbio, some of the world's most beautiful "Faenza" ceramics were thrown by his antecedents.

Luca had invited her to come to his cousin's wedding a few months later in Genova. It was close to the site of their first kiln after moving from Umbria to Liguria over 400 years ago.

She'd chosen to stay in Rapallo. She loved the rugged Liguria coastline and close by was the famous Portofino. A rich hunting ground either for uncomplicated sex or for her prey. For though she thoroughly enjoyed Luca's company and his body, she'd not had the urge to take his last breath.

Now, in the late August sun, she was spread out on her lounger by the hotel pool bar. She stood and stretched; aware her body was drawing lustful eyes from faces all around her. She deliberately bent from the waist to pick up her glass, she walked like a lazy cat, lithe and slinky.

She was a vision in her 50's style bikini, her rich auburn hair with its natural waves was piled carelessly on her head showing off her long swanlike neck. The perfect body, displaying raw sexuality yet still holding a whisper of innocence in her large violet blue eyes. Women and men lusted after her or were envious of her ample charms.

She returned with her refilled wine glass, executing a bunny-dip she slipped it under the edge of the lounger, turned and dived elegantly into the water. Her exit up the pool steps fifty lengths later reminded men of Ursula Andress in the Bond movie, "Dr No," and they shifted uncomfortably.

Lena was meeting Luca in Sori, a beautiful clifftop village to the east. She was sipping a rich red and watching a ship; it might have been straight from the "Onedin Line" television programme. With a full complement of billowing sails, the sun setting on the horizon, and the heady aroma of orange and Jasmine growing everywhere, she'd let her mind drift. Thus distracted she didn't see his approach, his breath on the back of her neck a second before his lips announced his arrival, she smiled.

Hours later, lying satisfied in his arms, he was giving her details of the venue, offering to collect her. She declined she had her reasons. She never went anywhere without in-depth research. The photo of the bride to be, had sparked something she'd thought had been a passing phase from her teen years, her first girl crush. However, her reaction to this beautiful woman was very familiar. She wasn't gay, or was she? Or was she just discovering another facet of her personality. Let's face it she thought, it's no ordinary personality!

She laughed at these thoughts and the possibilities it presented.

Something in Luca's last few words brought her to full attention.

"My cousin is a lucky man, but I'm astonished, he's a red-blooded Italian male, yet he seems unperturbed by her liaisons with other women. Gino says, "It's not really adultery is it?" "However, I have a feeling he is a bit of a player and voyeurism wouldn't be a shock. I mean most men fantasise about it. Anyway, I thought it prudent to appraise you of her tastes, just in case!"

She played her slightly shocked look and lowered her lashes. Luca left shortly after, leaving her with lots to think about.

Ten days later, she'd been busy. She'd discovered Angelica's favourite coffee shops and had instigated conversation over an expresso. Angelica's eyes had appraised Lena thoroughly, what she saw was, a white blonde head of gentle waves, striking green eyes and a boyish frame. Exactly as Lena had planned., peroxide had achieved the hair, coloured contact lenses changed her eyes, a strong band across her breast gave her a flatter look.

A south African accent completed her transformation.

Now with five days left before the big day, Lena's plans were coming together. They'd been seen in the cafés, bars and restaurants in various small villages to the north east of Modena, and their affection for each other had been left in no doubt.

The day of the wedding dawned bright and clear over Genova. Guests were to begin arriving at about eleven for the noon service in the beautiful 16th century castle, Santa Margherita Ligure.

Lena had returned her hair and eye colour to her luscious auburn and violet blue. She also had dropped the accent and used the English one Luca was familiar with.

She'd reconnoitred the stunning castle and had found the perfect spot. She sent a text to Angelica to meet her in an ante chamber before she dressed for the ceremony.

Angelica entered and the door closed behind her. She turned, confused, she knew the woman before her, yet she almost didn't recognise her, she bore barely a fleeting resemblance of the woman she'd spent so much time with, who had been her lover.

Lena placed her hand on Angie's delicately tinted cheek, then entwined her fingers in her long almost black tresses, pulling her head towards her. Their lips at first gentle, but Lena was practiced at raising the temperature. Her tongue probed and flicked into Angelica's mouth. A low moan escaped her. Lena's hands were doing magical work on all Angie's weak spots.

She didn't see or feel the prick of the needle as Lena bit her neck just above the needle. Realisation then terror were swift to appear in Angelica's eyes. Lena lowered her languid form to the floor. Still kissing her neck and cheek she whispered, "Sleep babes, sleep, it's time to say good-bye."

A small sigh was all that marked Angelica's departure from this life. Lena took her lover's mobile and threw it deftly out of the window onto the first truck that passed below heading east.

Quickly then she lifted the trap door, it was used in days of yore to dispose of effluence, dropping directly down a stone flue into the Adriatic. It would be days if ever before her body washed up.

Lena slipped unseen into the main hall area and entered the ladies powder room. Composed she returned to the bar; she'd been gone less than 15 minutes. Luca found her sitting on the terrace, "Where were you?" he said kissing her cheek.

"I came out to enjoy the view after going to powder my nose, did you miss me?"

He kissed her hard on the lips, it was just getting interesting when a male voice called out.

"Luca, a moment please."

It was Luca's friend and Gino's best man, Giuliano, she heard him whisper, "She's stood him up."

"What, oh God, is he okay, where is she?" Luca asked in a hushed voice.

Giuliano replied, "She's gone, not a word, and she's not answering her phone!"

"What do we do?" asked Luca.

"I'm just going to announce that the wedding is off!"

"Do you want me to stay?" Lena and I can help maybe?"

"No, my friend, take your English rose back to Rapallo, have a good dinner and I'll call you tomorrow. I will take Gino for food then make sure he is okay tonight."

They left, their meal was eaten alfresco, they had driven out to Reco and enjoyed some wine before Luca took her to her hotel. They spent a night of passion then early the next morning Luca drove her to the airport.

She kissed him good-bye at the drop-off point, waving till he was out of sight. She then took a taxi to the railway station and bought a ticket for Florence. Some wine, culture and pasta before she flew home.

She smiled at the thought of Luca, a lovely memory, it would warm her thoughts on many a night to come.

Part Four - So Close!

Any moment now, accompanied by the headmaster, the new teacher was due to join them in the staff room.

She was vaguely aware of a frisson of excitement coming from a gaggle of middle-aged spinsters who taught years 4, 5, and 6. She'd have rated her curiosity at about one on a scale of one to one hundred. She returned her attention to her book. That rating changed to one hundred and one as the newcomer turned to say hi to everyone.

Fraser was led into the staffroom by Mr Jempson, the head of St Elizabeth's Catholic school on the Isle of Lindisfarne off the coast of Northumberland. Calum was aware of the flurry of interest his entrance made, but apart from some girlish type giggling from an older woman who taught art, the welcome was warm and friendly. Except that is from one woman.

Beautiful, she was, elegant, she was, friendly, she was not. Her attitude was more glacial than gracious, not that that bothered him.

Fraser Robertson had spent the best part of ten years with the army, he'd demobbed after the death of his older brother. His parents hadn't coped well, and Fraser went home to help his father on their smallholding. It didn't end as he'd hoped. His mother, destroyed by grief after the loss of her firstborn son, took her own life eighteen months after he'd left The Regiment.

He'd been headhunted, his Argyll & Sutherland Highlanders commanding officer had called him into his office early one morning. He smiled proudly at Calum,

"Laddie you've been invited to try for "The Regiment," are you game?"

"Of course, Sir, be honoured to, though I'd be sad to leave the lads here."

He'd gone on to travel the world with these men from Hereford, who also become like brothers to him.

But there was no other choice than to return home after his brother's death. His five years apiece with two of the greatest regiments in the land was over. It took him another three years to decide on his next career move.

His father had developed early onset dementia, and Calum hated farming. So, he sold the farm after finding a superb facility for folk like his father.

Fraser spent hours researching his next mission as he called it. It took a year before he'd made any headway. Then overnight everything changed gear. Two separate responses to his appeals for videos or photos taken in specific locations in Aberdeen, Edinburgh and a couple of European locations, all within a specific timeframe, had come in together. At last a trail. The two items of footage had shown up some interesting faces. He'd then asked a favour of an old army buddy, now serving in the Met, with his help, they'd struck lucky with the facial recognition software, that the police use now. Both films put the same face in the relevant places at the relevant times for his theory to hold up.

Now he needed to track the whereabouts of what the police refer to as the "person of interest," he was most assuredly interested. Finally, he'd found her, at least he believed he had

Two other contacts from his time in the army who were on the force, but way high up, had managed to pull some strings and they'd set a plan in motion. Fraser trained for eight weeks with his two pals in special ops and some other men, at the end of the gruelling training, they believed he could pull it off and sanction was given for the plan to go ahead. He then did a crash course in teacher training and then was off.

Now here he was, and she was playing it cool, virtually ignoring him. He wasn't fooled though: he'd seen the moment of shock when he'd turned and said "hi." The resemblance was quite marked, he knew she was curious if nothing else.

Fraser avoided the staffroom when he was alone, he usually flirted and teased the art mistress, it cheered her lonely days. He'd learnt that she alone cared for her elderly mother, it was all in light-hearted humour, but it put a smile on her face, and a bounce in her step, if only for a short time.

As I was saying, he avoided any opportunities for Ms Hyde to instigate conversation. Oh, he knew she'd wanted to, on a good few occasions she'd made to join him, but either someone else had gotten to him first, or he'd avoided her by joining another group, or on one occasion went to the men's room.

Her frustration was rising by the minute. Never, not once in her entire life, had a man ignored her or been oblivious to her charms. It not only confused and irritated her, now it was beginning to undermine her self-esteem. She decided a different tack was required.

Next morning in front of the headmaster she approached Fraser head on.

"Hello Mr Robertson, look I know this might be a tad forward, but I've tickets for the Ceilidh at the castle on Saturday. I was thinking if you'd like to join me, it might give you the opportunity to meet some other people than just us in the school, you being new on the island."

He was on the spot, just as she'd planned, Mr Jempson answered for him. "Ms Hyde, Lena, I think that's a wonderful idea, don't you Fraser? Sure, it'll be a great craic as our Irish cousins would say. Of course, he'll go Lena, and thank you, I should have thought of something myself."

Fraser turned, he knew she was interested, and he wasn't oblivious to her beauty, she was a stunner.

"I'd be delighted, Lena is it?

"Yes, it's Lena, how do you do," she put out her slender, beautifully manicured hand and shook his. It was a firm hand that exuded cool confidence. She's a rare one, I'll give her that.

He smiled, reached into his top pocket and handed her a card, my number's on there, text me the address, I'll pick you up."

"No need, it has your address on here, I'll pick you up at 6 p.m. Saturday."

"No Lena, I'll come to your concert or whatever you called it, but I'm not young enough to use the new dating rules. I'll pick you up at six, and I'll pay for supper or I'm not coming."

She was furious, no-one was ever allowed to her home, and especially she didn't want this man anywhere near it, but she was stuck.

"Very well, I'll text you later."

She walked away, unaware of the satisfied smile on his face.

Fraser called Commander Baxter, "She's made her move. The Ceilidh at the castle, Saturday next. I'll be in touch."

"Go careful old chap" Calum rung off.

He collected her on the dot of 6 p.m. As he pulled up outside her cottage about a half a mile outside town, the door opened. She came out, locking the door behind her. No invite in then Calum thought in amusement.

Soft cornflower blue jumper, stone washed jeans, boots and a shawl, her hair loose and wavy. She was beautiful.

As they drove along Chare Ends and onto Marygate and then the coast road to the castle, they chatted easily. He was impressed by her, she was intelligent, witty and interesting, he saw her power, he liked her, he didn't like that.

Lena was watching him as he drove, he responded without hesitation to her barrage of questions on family, "where was he born?"

"Orkney Isles," he replied.

Nowhere near she thought with relief. And he was funny and had a quirky way of viewing some things, she liked him, and she didn't like that.

Over dinner she asked where he'd trained, when he qualified, how he'd come so late to teaching, what did he do before? He answered in easy measured tones. Time in the forces, went travelling, then he said he'd cared for his elderly parents, now deceased, (a small half lie, he figured it was safe enough) Then he said he'd decided to try teaching, and so now, here he was."

He made inquiries of similar sorts and she'd seemed at ease.

"Born in London's suburbs, parents also dead, no siblings, moved north after a holiday where she'd spotted an ad for a teacher needed here, and so here she was."

He knew every word was a lie.

She'd been born and raised in Brighton in an orphanage, parents had abandoned her, and that was the kindest thing they'd ever done for her. She'd run away and did her training in Newcastle then came to Lindisfarne directly from there. That was near to her truth, he was sure there was more to it than that.

The Ceilidh was wonderful, the musicians were skilled and had showmanship too. They'd danced and had a couple of glasses of the local brew. They were very easy in each other's company. Afterwards they went to a wonderful Italian bistro, small, cosy and served great food. They enjoyed each other and the food.

As they left, she slid her arm through his as they headed for the car.

"Shall we walk a little, get a bit of air?" he suggested.

"That'd be lovely," she said, resting her head on his shoulder as they walked. The path to the headland where the view of the sea, the subtle lighting that lit the castle, created a very romantic setting. It wasn't wasted by either of them.

It's going as planned he thought, reel her in, gain her trust, then get the evidence.

She stood with her back to him taking in the moonlight as it played on the turbulent water. He moved in behind her, as she'd anticipated. I'll ensnare him, then he'll go back to the farm, at least that's what the letter I take into school, broken hearted after the school have learnt we've been seeing each other and have fallen in love.

And whoever he is, he'll be swimming with the fishes. She smiled, she loved that line from her favourite movie.

He stood, her back inches in front of him, his hands leaning on the railings either side of her, looking out to sea. Smiling, she turned inside his arms,

"Shall we head back to the other side of town, there's a good pub just twenty minutes' walk from my place."

That sounded like an invitation he thought, he was shocked to realise the thought excited him. "Sounds good to me, lead the way."

It was a fine old pub, lots of atmosphere, beams and an open log fire. He went to the bar.

"A large Tanqueray 10 gin please" he'd said in reply to the barman's question of,

"What's your poison?"

It was new to Fraser, very much a beer and chaser man.

"So is this some new-fangled drink for toffs," he'd asked as he sat down.

"NO, it's been around since 1830, what a provincial thing you are. I'm surprised, especially for one so well-travelled."

He laughed,

"Yep, just a common foot soldier Ma'am."

"I doubt there's anything common about you,"

she said as she looked up through long black lashes, her eyes held promises he knew he should avoid, but Lord if she wasn't intoxicating.

He called it a night after two, he had to drive back to his digs. They'd left the car near Lena's cottage. He was grateful for the chill of refreshing cool night air it was just what he needed to keep a clear head. As they reached the cottage, he let her get her key in the door, and using the moment, said, over his shoulder,

"G'night Lena, and thanks. I had a good time, see you Monday."

He knew she'd had other plans for tonight, but he would be controlling each and every move, despite her best intentions and bewitching charms.

Lena was dumbfounded when Fraser had so abruptly left for home as she was busy with the key. She knew he was interested, the same way every woman knows when a man is. It had burned in his eyes off and on all evening. There was no denying the electricity between them when they touched. She could wait, she hadn't wanted to, she was eager to bed this handsome, intelligent man, who so painfully reminded her of the other man. The only man she felt she could ever have truly loved. He was dead now, so no point dwelling on it, but sometimes the loneliness enveloped her, and she regretted not exploring that relationship. Water under the bridge she chastised herself. This one would fall at her feet and be her lover, for how long, well now, that was a whole other matter.

Over the following few weeks Fraser was friendly but busy. He was away both weekends, a friend's wedding, a party for an aging aunt's 80th birthday. Hence, he saw Lena only at school.

She had suggested supper one evening, he'd cried off stating he had some paperwork to get done for an upcoming test he was setting his class. She was intrigued by him, but he also frustrated all her plans and evaded her company. Then after two and a half weeks, he caught her alone in the staffroom.

Coming up silently behind her, softly kissing the exposed nape of her neck,

"Been wanting to do that for ages now" he whispered in her ear.

She'd frozen when his lips brushed the skin of her neck, shocked by her body's response, and her mental one too if she was honest. She didn't need him to know that.

"Oh, what, at a loose end are you? I'm sure I can't imagine why you'd think it ok to take such liberties. I'll thank you to not be so forward!"

"Oh, Lena, please, let's not play games. I'd been given licence to do much more than that when I dropped you at your place a fortnight ago." He pulled her swiftly into his arms and kissed her.

Though ravaged her mouth might be a more accurate description. He let her go just as abruptly. Laughing, he left the room. Lena stood rooted to the spot, heart racing, her body in meltdown, and her mind firing off all kinds of warnings. Oh my, this will be interesting she thought.

As Fraser headed from their encounter to his car, his heart was pounding, he was exhilarated, his body wanted her, his mind gave him licence to enjoy her body, but he knew this was dangerous. It would be interesting though he thought. However, the reason he was here still ruled every move he made. He needed to be careful, she was very moreish.

Over the next five, or six months things carried on in much the same vein, a game of cat and mouse. She'd move closer, he'd back away. Then he'd raise the tempo, then cool it down.

Then, one day they'd gone rock climbing. Lena had said she'd done some before when he suggested it, it was old hat for him.

It was a beautiful autumn day, they'd gone over to the mainland to Bowden Doors, that would get the adrenalin flowing he mused.

They'd barely reached a point of about twenty-five feet up when he realised, she was in trouble. Before he could do anything, she'd made a rookie mistake and fell. Her safety harness stopped her crashing to the ground below, but she'd clattered against the rock face on more than one occasion, and hard.

She was hanging limp. He reached her in just a few minutes and lowering her gently to the ground he checked her out. She was going to have a duck-egg sized contusion on her temple and her left arm was badly broken. After immobilising her arm, he lay her gently on the back seat of his jeep and took off driving at speed the eighteen miles to Alnwick Infirmary.

Five hours later she was sitting up in the AAU ward, arm in a cast and a large bump above her right eye, which was turning all shades of blue, black and yellow. She looked pale but was chirpy for all that.

"My own fault," she'd said, "I shouldn't have lied, but I wanted to impress. It never occurred to me you'd pick such a difficult climb. I've only been once, an intro to rock climbing at a community college."

She looked down and he realised she was crying, "I'm sorry Fraser, it was stupid."

He was astonished to find himself feeling sorry for her. "Okay, but no more lies, okay?"

She was quiet for about five minutes than very quietly she said,

"Then I need to 'fess up'."

Laughing, he asked, "what for?"

She then began with something he really didn't expect.

"My real name was Lorna, my parents were junkies, my father used me, and in exchange for drugs, let his friends use me too. My mother wanted her share of these drugs but was jealous and was viciously cruel to me after my father had begun raping me. They did one singularly kind thing, they dumped me in an orphanage and never came back. The Catholic priests and nuns were so kind, I thrived under their care. I was often used as the poster girl for the good that the church does. The fact that one or two of the priests also wanted to use my lithe teenage body, barely registered at the time."

"They didn't hurt me, brought me gifts."

"Not for years did I realise they were worse in a way than my parents. They had been drug addled, they'd lost all their humanity in the fog of heroin or crack, and the need for more."

"The Fathers had no such excuse."

"Anyway, if it's no more lies from me, you needed to hear that. I left the orphanage at eighteen. I trained in York to be a teacher and came here straight from college. That's the real me."

The tears had been gaining momentum and now sobs racked her body. He hadn't realised he'd moved, yet he found himself sat on her bed, holding her as she wept.

"I've never told another living soul before," she gulped, "I'm so sorry, Fraser, with you I'm a different person, as if I'm being allowed to be the woman of full potential I was born to be."

He stroked her hair, he felt genuine sympathy for her, this woman who'd taken the life of his brother.

"You need to sleep, rest now. I'll be back in tomorrow to see how you are"

He squeezed her hand and got the hell out of there. He'd been so tempted to kiss her.

I need a drink, he thought, climbing into the jeep.

Fraser arrived at the hospital next day only to be told she'd discharged herself just after six the previous evening. He stood, bouquet in hand, feeling confused, gauche and angry with himself. He'd blown it. He drove dangerously fast to her cottage, there was no reply as he beat a tattoo on her heavy oak door for over ten minutes. He then called the headmaster.

"Hello Mr Jenkins, Fraser here,"

"Oh, please don't tell me you're leaving too, though I did suspect it might be the case. I hadn't heard from you all day, so still had some hope till now."

"What do you mean?" Fraser almost shouted.

"Lena resigned her post by email last night, effective immediately, she said she'd had an offer abroad that she couldn't turn down. I thought you might be going with her."

"Did she leave a forwarding address? We had a spat last night and I want to make things right," Fraser held his breath, in a last dying breath of hope.

"No, son, she didn't. Told me to donate her pay owed to a children's charity. Sorry, son."

Fraser drove back to his flat, anger threatening to overwhelm him, aimed at himself, he should have focused more. He felt like a fluff-faced youth. She'd bolted, she'd played him.

He wouldn't give up his quest, but she'd cover her tracks more carefully now, it would take a miracle.

Five years had passed when Calum saw the headline in his news feed:

"Woman's body washes up on Miami beach"

As he read on, the hairs on the back of his neck prickled. He took a flight into Miami the following day. The headlines had read.

"Woman found is believed to be a Lena Hyde-Robertson," according the Dade County Sheriff's Office. A British passport was found in a hotel room less than a mile away. The guest fitting the description had not returned to her room for two nights. She'd last been seen with another woman, who also has not been seen since, but who had not been staying at the hotel where the passport was found. Due to the condition of the body, identification would prove difficult without a DNA match...

He needed to see the body.

As he alighted the Yellow cab a greyhound bus passed by, a blonde woman turned, her brain challenging the statement of her eyes. The eyes had it, she smiled, it was good to see Fraser looking so well. She was delighted that he still looked for her.

Malachai Murphy had watched her sway and weave through the bustling market crowd. She was a vision to equal Aphrodite's legendary beauty. Long rich auburn locks of wavy loose curls hung to her slender waist. Her complexion a perfect alabaster with cheeks that held a hint of pale pink blush. She'd turned many a head as she sashayed from stall to stall. He'd headed to the restaurant where she took coffee every morning about ten a.m. Over the previous week they'd begun to nod and smile when either arrived. He had made it his business to ensure he was there first for the last five days and that day was the day he'd determined to make his move. He let his mind unfold the memory.

"Buongiorno senorina" he'd given his best dimpled smile; it had rarely failed to get him to first base with the ladies. And he'd used it unashamedly since his teenage years back in Cork, southern Ireland. His deep twinkling blue eyes, black hair and that dimpled smile was legend. Many a lass had cried when they'd learnt that Malachai was leaving his native land to travel. Italy was where he was now.

Murphy had been in the army, then in the local Garda, but Cork was too parochial, and he was restless. So, when he was invited to attend an interview with Interpol, he'd made sure their assessment that he was a great cop, was on the money.

He had just finished an intensive debrief after some tricky undercover work. It had been a long six months and the threat by a splinter IRA group that they'd "See you later boyo" had earned him a month's leave. He'd come to Italy; within a fortnight he'd asked for a temporary transfer. When his boss had heard his reasoning, it was sanctioned, along with his plan.

She caught his eye one morning towards the end of his first week. He'd been out for a morning stroll, looking for a place to get breakfast and a much-needed coffee. She was sitting with her fashionable Hepburn style sunglasses perched at the end of a perfect aquiline nose, her large wide brimmed hat flopped down over her brow yet left her beauty undiminished. He'd sat at a table adjacent. She'd looked up and shamelessly surveyed him, like he was a horse she thought to buy.

Her last affair of the heart had ended badly, and for a year or more she'd satisfied her lust with uncomplicated one-night stands. Her nature, however, demanded more, much more. When she'd seen him, she knew he was the one to sate the growing demand for real satisfaction.

As she'd approached the Café' Napoli, she spotted him. He lazily scanned the crowd. He had the demeanour of a relaxed tiger and she could sense his power: she knew he could strike at a moment's notice. That his prey would be a beautiful woman and his weapons that glorious dimple and those captivating blue eyes mattered little. He would still be lethal. She'd bet many a heart had been stopped, even if only momentarily, caught in the crosshairs of his devastating smile.

He'd been brazen in his appraisal as she'd approached. She laughed aloud at his impudence as she entered the framed area of outside tables. He stood as she headed his way. He pulled the other chair at his table out, and with a theatrical flourish of hand and head, he invited her to sit with him. She introduced herself as Lorena.

Their conversation and laughter had flowed through the sunny morning, then lunch, and by the time they left, aperitifs for dinner were being called for. He casually draped his arm over her shoulder as he steered her towards his hotel a street away, she made no protest.

His room had an amazing view of the Bay of Napoli and the ancient draped four poster bed made the perfect setting for seduction, but who was seducing whom?

Malachai was no innocent, and she was a very desirable woman, but it didn't come easy to make love to a woman like this. He was inherently an honest and decent man and lovemaking meant something in his private life, so these trysts never sat easy with Malachai.

They'd made love late into the night and slept till late morning. They stayed in his room until early evening, using room service for brunch. By the evening, hunger for something more substantial forced them to rise and shower. At about eight they returned to Cafe Napoli.

Large plates of *impepata di cozze* were brought to be table. The bay ensured the most fabulous seafood, freshly caught daily. Mussels in olive oil, tomatoes, red chillies, white wine, and parsley, with crusty bread, washed down with *Nanni Cope*, a great red from Campania. The *zabaglione*, with its rich Marsala flavoured frothy custard ended their meal perfectly. Still laughing and talking they headed back to his room.

She'd thought it sweet that he'd called his "Ma" as they waited for dessert. He'd been jocular and easy as he ended the short call to let her know he'd "Found heaven" and had to go as he said he was Hhoping to sleep in the arms of an angel."

She could hear the feminine chuckle and what she thought an admonishment as the woman called him an "*Amadan Dubh*." She was unaware of its meaning.

A dark fool or fairy trickster in the Gaelic.

He stopped at the door of his room and kissed her soundly then twirled her away from him, propelling her through the doorway. She landed, still laughing, in the arms of two waiting officers from Interpol.

Lorna Feeney, (for that was her real name) climbed the steps, and as she walked into the room, a hush fell over the crowded court. In her direct line of vision sat Malachai and his old friend from the "Regiment," Fraser Robertson. In unison they saluted her as the long list of charges were read, including the name of Fraser's brother Calum.

Neither man noticed the old woman as she hobbled forward into the courtroom. The report of the pistol drew their eyes to her. She was dropped in a volley of shots by trained police. Malachi knelt by the dying woman. She smiled up at him and said, "She murdered my only son, now I go to join him, and she goes back to her father the devil." Lorna was already dead from a well-placed, albeit lucky, shot right between her now-unseeing eyes.

The old woman sighed and died.

Later Malachi and Fraser shared a beer and chewed over the day's events. The old woman was the mother of one of the "vacation killer's" victims. The poor woman had been in and out of psychiatric wards since her son's death. The photos in the global press had moved her to act. Fraser shared his mixed feeling of relief, that it was truly over, and Calum's killer had paid for her crime. Yet there was also disappointment that her punishment was less painful and drawn out than the life sentences of grieving that she'd left her victims' families with.

The two old friends made their goodbyes through very bleary eyes in the wee small hours.

The saga of the murderous siren was over.

Novella Four: The Hibernian

Part One: The Gift

The letter had arrived last month. Her great-aunt over in Canada, with whom she had only loosely kept in touch, had died and had left her a bequest in her will. Jeannie was on her way to a local solicitor, who was acting as proxy for her aunt in Calgary.

Two hours later she emerged from Stollen and Cash in utter confusion. Her aunt had left her everything... There was a caveat, however. To claim it all, she must travel to her aunt's home as there were things her aunt had organised to be collected in person.

One angry boss and two weeks later Jeannie stepped out of the cab beside a beautiful two-story house in the leafy suburb of Alberta's largest city. It was a quaint house with white picket fence and spacious wraparound porch, (a secret desire of Jeannie's). The dark rose-coloured door was surrounded with a well-trained wisteria, wrapped like a bower over the frame.

Inside was a lovely light space with solid wood furniture, the walls washed in a soft shade of yellow. It made you want to curl up and grab one of the many books which filled the large bookcase along one wall.

On the huge dining table stood an envelope addressed to her, along with a small package. As she read the letter, she didn't know whether to laugh or cry. Poor Aunt Tilly, she obviously had begun to suffer some form of dementia. The letter was a flight of fancy in anyone's book.

Jeannie opened the box: inside lay a beautiful chain with an intricate design and hanging at the end, a ring. It was such a very unusual design, the marcasite really made it something special. The facets of the dark emerald held the surprises of this delightful prism.

She slipped the chain over her riot of titian hair, a gift from her Hibernian ancestors, along with sharp blue eyes the shade of quality sapphires. The other inheritance from her ancestors was *the GIFT*. She occasionally had insights of the future, "So much for that, I didn't see this coming," she thought aloud. Oddly enough, Aunt Tilly was supposed to have had the gift too.

Jeannie found the kitchen, made herself some tea and curled up in one of the comfy sofas to reread the letter, it really was mind boggling.

In a nutshell, her aunt's letter said that the ring would take her to any moment in time. She had but to slip it on and repeat the phrase written in the ancient Gaelic, a language that predates the Boudicca uprising in England and the Pictish invasion of Alba.

The instructions for use were simple, however the ethical directions were more complex: "*Bring nothing back from the past to enhance your material wealth, and take only organic things into the past with which to do good.*"

She looked at the clock and was astonished to discover she'd spent almost two hours running scenarios through her head to circumvent these instructions. She laughed out loud, "As if I could really time travel… insane!"

After she'd unpacked her case and made herself some dinner, Jeannie was surprised by a knock at the door. Wearing loose palazzo pants and an oversized jumper she opened the door to find a rather serious and dishevelled looking man whose sudden smile changed the whole impression of him instantly. In a thick Irish brogue, he laughingly said, "Well you look just like yer auntie for sure, so you do."

Jeannie was mortified. She was twenty-seven; her aunt was ninety-eight when she'd passed. This rogue was her age, so how could he determine such a personal assessment in the few moments since she opened the door. He had no idea how much danger he was in, for at home Jeannie's temper and sharp tongue was infamous within her circle.

He smiled again. "Ah sure don't take on so me darlin', that aunt of yours was a glorious Celtic beauty in her youth. Did you never see the pictures of her? Well, are you going to stand there bristling all night or are you about to show you know how Irish hospitality works?"

"What do you want and who are you?" Jeannie spluttered; she was furious at the cheek of him.

"Ah, now I see why we've gotten off on the wrong foot here, and I am sorry for that. I am Liam, good friend of your aunt's. She asked that I came over tonight, she thought you'd be needing some help to get your head round her gift." He dared a sidelong glance at Jeannie, she didn't seem any calmer now.

"And how and what do you know of her gift?" Jeannie growled, her hands closed into a tight fist.

"Let's sit down and I'll tell you, lassie, though I doubt that you'll be believing me tonight."

Hours later she sat in shocked disbelief at his story.

Liam had spun her a yarn of a 17th century battle and how Tilly had made her first journey through time to the edge of the battlefield by the River Boyne near Drogheda. How he, Liam, had lain seriously injured and although he'd crawled to a place of cover, he was losing blood fast. He knew he'd be food for the wolves soon enough. Tilly had appeared from nowhere, though at the time he thought her a figment of his dying mind. She had swiftly bound his wound and he'd passed out as she tried to get him to his feet. He said, when he'd come to, he was lying on the same couch Jeannie was perched upon.

No matter which way she asked the questions, Liam stood firm on the details of his story of their many time-travel exploits over eighty-two years. His heritage was from the fairy folk, hence his still young appearance and his longevity. She heard herself ask, "Did she bring others back?"

"No, I was the only one. I was her soulmate, as she was mine, but that wasn't why. The fates allowed me to time travel with her because the ring keeper must have a skilled warrior as her guardian on her travels. I was Tilly's, and my life - like hers - is almost done, I shall live only long enough to deliver you to your warrior. Well now, lassie, I'll away and leave you to get some sleep. I'll be seeing you soon. Goodnight."

Still a little distracted by her own thoughts, she muttered "goodnight" and he was gone before she realised she had no idea how to contact him.

Jeannie had a long soak in Tilly's huge roll top bath and pondered the events of the last few hours. She didn't believe it was possible to time travel, but how could she challenge Liam's reality if she didn't try the ring and the chant. She picked up the letter and box, the words she was meant to repeat, if she donned the ring, were in Gaelic, she'd no idea how to pronounce the strange phrase.

I gcas ina bhfuil ag I eastail, tigherna a chosaint dom, agus a chonneail, me ar ais go dti mo ait chui. Tilly had written the English translation beneath it, "Where ere I'm needed, Lord protect me and keep me safe, return me to my proper place."

She read them over and over again; each time the cadence and rhythm felt more familiar in her head. Ah well, she thought, here goes nothing. She grabbed her pen and pad and wrote a note. I'm following in Tilly's footsteps, she wanted Liam to see this and she also took out her phone and selected the camcorder setting. She set it on the bedside cabinet and videoed herself.

Removing the ring from the box, she smiled at the camera and said "tally-ho" and repeated the chant aloud, feeling very foolish for the split second before everything went into a tailspin.

When she regained consciousness, she was shocked to see Liam sitting beside her as a sixteenth century warrior, beside him stood an Adonis of a man in the uniform of a Roman centurion. Liam introduced the centurion as *Gracus Aurelius*, your guardian. Jeannie fainted.

Part Two: The Arrival

When Jeannie came to, she was looking up into the darkest of brown eyes. Behind the left ear that belonged to the owner of these amber orbs, stood Liam. He looked anxious, but more shocking to her was that he looked old, tired, and the grey in his hair more than whispered of him being an elder. He smiled at her, "Now don't be frettin' ma girl, it's near my time to join that Amazon that was your great-aunt." He turned to go, heading towards a copse about a one thousand yards away.

She leapt to her feet, "Liam, wait, you can't leave me here all alone!" He turned slowly, "Ah now darlin', but you're not alone at all, sure isn't Gracus here to guide and protect you?"

He continued on towards the trees. She was so scared she felt her bladder threaten to shame her. She turned, Gracus knelt on one knee, "*Domina*, I am your servant, all that I am and can be, I offer you. I will protect you, even unto my last breath and with my body shield you if that is all I have to hand. It is my honour to have been chosen as your guardian."

"Well then, just get me home, to my time, I cannot do this time travelly thing, I just want to go home." She sat down heavily on a fallen tree trunk, her face buried in her hands.

As Gracus began to speak, the air was rent by blood-curdling screams an instant before the treeline erupted with about a dozen or so woad faced fearsome devils who were racing towards them. Jeannie saw Liam draw his sword and the last words she heard from him was "Gracus, Go, NOW."

Before she could compute his words, she was swung over Gracus's back and he was racing towards a small boat that was barely visible under an overhanging tree on the river. This leviathan of a soldier was rowing before she'd had time to blink. She looked back, straining to see, and there was Liam the great warrior. Three men lay near the right hand wielding sword of this dedicated protector. There were too many, though, and she held her breath as she saw four of them charge him together, and still held it even after she'd seen Liam fall. She was sobbing as Gracus pulled aside some foliage and drew the boat into a shallow cave, if you hadn't known it was there, you'd have missed it for certain.

Later, when Gracus had made a lone recce of the area and deemed it now safe to leave, they returned to where Liam had fought such a brave rear guard action to save them. Five blue painted bodies now lay beside Liam's body. With surprising tenderness for a man of his build, Gracus lifted the limp and lifeless body and carried Liam to where the small boat was tethered. After gathering some twigs and then larger sticks of wood they filled the bottom of the boat, he topped them with a weave of moss and leaves. Then he threw his *lacerna* (cloak) over it all. He lifted Liam and laid him on this facsimile of a bed, then from a pack Jeannie hadn't noticed before he drew a flask and poured the contents over the wood and Liam.

"Say goodbye to a guardian of your family."

Jeannie, as if exiting a coma, realised then what he'd been doing. She stood and from her jeans pocket, pulled her lighter, lit it, and dropped it into the boat, it was an ill-fitted pyre for such a man. Gracus stared in awe at the flame carrier as he called it. She sat down and wept. "I want to go home," she whispered in anguish.

Gracus moved to kneel at her feet, "then repeat your words and we'll be there. Might I ask, *Domina*, where exactly is home to you and what is it like there?"

Jeannie looked at this hardened Roman warrior, "Have you travelled before Gracus?"

"No, this will be my first assignment, as the only man known to survive from the 9th Legion. I was chosen but days ago."

"Oh Lord," she thought, "how do I explain 2017 to a soldier from AD 120?" A small voice in her head said, "Don't even try," so she didn't.

She spoke the words in the Gaelic and the whirring in her head began again.

When she awakened, she was lying in the arms of this very buff soldier in his Roman uniform. Her mind, at least momentarily, was not focused on disentangling herself from this, warm, safe, and very attractive spot.

He came to, shaking his head as if shaking water from his hair, when he opened his eyes, Jeannie, in that instant, saw the one and only display of fear he ever was to show.

"Be calm Gracus, we are in my time, and if I'm not hallucinating all this, then we need to get you acclimatised, and we'll start with the clothes."

As she stood she spotted an envelope on the table, it was addressed to her, she read the contents in amazement, Aunt Tilly had seen this time and her note said that Liam had shopped for him and everything to get Gracus settled initially is in the spare room.

Jeannie let out an almost hysterical sounding laugh and looking to Gracus said, "Okay, soldier, well it looks like we're in for some adventures together. Follow me!" and he did, and she loved that he did… The arrival of Gracus in her life was going to be interesting she mused.

Gracus was glowering, again. Jeannie always found it amusing to extract his frustration with her refusal to obey his random commands. This time, however, she knew she must bow to his martial superiority.

60 AD she knew was the year Prasutagus, King of the Iceni, died. And from all she could gather from Gracus's summation of their current location, they were watching the Roman legion advancing upon the residence of Prasutagus's family, and his Queen, Boadicia or Boudica. They were somewhere on the east coast area of England.

Jeannie had read the stories of Boudica's rebellion against Rome, and the terrible price she and her children paid for standing against the unjust seizing of the land of her people. Her husband had tried to safeguard them by splitting the ruling of the tribe between Boudica and the Roman Legate. Rome's greed was unsatisfied.

Gracus motioned for her to move further back into the wood overlooking the homes of the Iceni people.

Although a good distance from the Romans, he kept his voice low.

"We must leave here now, *Domina*, we can do no good."

Jeannie smiled and looked Gracus square in the eye saying, "Maybe, maybe not, but I have been sent to this exact time and place, so my being here has a purpose, we stay."

Although Jeannie and Gracus's relationship was still in its infancy, he knew the set of her jaw and the steel in her blue eyes. They would be staying.

She was his to guard, this was his life's work now. Chosen by higher powers he still did not fully understand, it was his mission. To love her though, was his heart's choice and he knew his life would only have meaning whilst she was part of it.

They dined on dry food and water that night, not to give away their position to anyone passing on the narrow dirt path that led through the wood. Sometime a while before dawn, Gracus, who had lain awake all night watching Jeannie, such a simple joy he took in being able to just watch her sleep, heard the noises he recognised as an attack by a centurion cohort. Almost 500 soldiers were attacking the Iceni Queen's camp.

Jeannie woke, alerted to the assault by a tender shake of Gracus's gentle hands. It fascinated her that hands that could wield the *gladius* with such fatal effect on an enemy could be so tender and gentle. She was finding his physical presence often caused her to catch her breath, just from his nearness. She knew if she was honest, she was falling hard for her magnificent legionary.

Smoke and flames could be seen. The killing had begun and women and children could be seen running in every direction in a vain attempt to escape the weight of Rome's wrath. She needed to get closer. She stood and began to follow the line of trees which curved down into the shallow valley to the homes now aflame. It was still dark but the fire's light illuminated the village and the carnage within. Jeannie could see legionaries cutting down any and all whom they encountered, man, woman, and child. No matter how old or young, no quarter was given, no mercy was expected. She felt the tears slide down her cheeks. Gracus moved on to a spot that had line of vision to the small market square, his hand squeezed her shoulder as her eyes focused on the scene that had caught Gracus's attention.

Three women, two young, maybe between seventeen and twenty-two, and an older woman whose bearing screamed breeding and royalty. Despite being viciously violated herself, and able to see the multiple violations of her two bound daughters, she uttered not a sound. Her eyes locked onto a point where her innocent children were living a hell never imagined in their young minds.

Jeannie was in no doubt that she was watching Boudica, Queen of the Iceni, who looked more royal and high bred than the prelate who watched her defilement. Jeannie wanted to kill him for his inhuman actions towards three female prisoners. What Boudica was feeling she could not imagine. As dawn broke, the Romans formed up and marched away carrying anything of any value or use, leaving only death, destruction, and a renewed hatred burning behind them.

As soon as they could safely do so, Jeannie and Gracus entered the village, immediately cutting down Boudica and her daughters, all three battered and bleeding from the multiple rapes. When Jeanie lifted Boudica's hand, this Amazon of a woman smiled and said "So Tilly's promise will be fulfilled."

Jeannie whilst shocked by these words, replied, "What do you mean and how do you know that name?"

"Ah, Tilly came many summers ago and promised that she, or her heir, would come to me in my darkest day and keep another promise to me."

They found a building still partially intact and gathered rags and bedding to let these women rest upon. Gracus brought in water and some wine to help revive those who were drifting back into the village in shock. Jeannie sat with Boudica, this courageous woman entranced her. "Can you tell me how you met Tilly?"

A short time later Jeannie knew the circumstances of their meeting. Tilly had affected an intervention at the difficult delivery of Boudica's oldest daughter, her actions had not only saved the infant, but also the woman's ability to carry a further child. Tilly had, for some unfathomable reason before she left, imparted to Boudica, the fate awaiting these children of the Iceni queen. That was the same day that Boudica had extracted a blood vow from Tilly. That today, either Tilly or her heir, would return to save her daughters who owed their very lives to Tilly. Jeannie was mystified. What could she possibly do to help, it was too late surely?

Jeannie carried bags of herbs with her now as she often needed to administer care in her travels. She made a brew of Burdock, nettle, and the basis for modern aspirin, willow. The first two would stem the blood loss and act as an anti-toxin against infection carried by these soldiers. After allowing the three some rest, to commune with each other as mother and daughters and as women, Jennie approached Boudica again.

"What promise must I keep for Tilly?"

The queen smiled. "You will take my daughters to the future and keep them there for a period of twelve moons. Then, Tilly said Rome will soften to the Iceni and to the people of Britain. You must then return them to the Iceni, so that even if in secret, the Iceni will not be wiped from the earth."

Jeannie's heart was pounding, she'd had explicit instructions from day one of this incredible adventure. She was forbidden to bring things to the past, except organic matter and she could bring nothing to the future to enrich her personal life. So why did Tilly make such a promise in contradiction to her explicit instructions.

Boudica smiled, leant forward, patting Jeannie's hand she told her to come. She led Jeannie to a huge oak tree, leaning far into the bowl she extracted a bundle wrapped in hide, it held something solid. She unwrapped this copper alloy tin and handed it to Jeannie. "Tilly said I was to give this to you."

She accepted the tin and opened it, inside she found a piece of wax paper with writing on it. Jeannie realised she was looking at a letter from her dead aunt. She moved to get the best light and began to read.

"Dearest girl,

How thrilled I am that you have taken up the challenge of being the ring keeper. How's your guide working out? I can tell you this, he will be with you forever, always with your best interests at heart. But right now, I think maybe you want to know about this promise versus my instructions. Well, humans are all made from natural matter and by helping them back to your time, you will not benefit from this in any financial way, it was all I could think of to save their lives. The Romans will soften their ruling hand on Britain after a year, and they can return where the Druids will wait for them at this tree, one year from today. They will be married to Boudica's daughters and ensure the survival of the Iceni tribe, even if in secret. You must act today whilst there is still the possibility for uncertain verifications of their death being accepted as fact in Rome.

All love child, from Tilly."

Jeannie looked up into the bruised and dirt-stained face of Boudica, she was smiling, "I know what the future holds and as a mother and a queen I cannot cast my daughters' lives away fruitlessly from selfish wish to hold them close to me. They must live, and if you do as Tilly planned, as a mother I can save my children and protect them from watching their mother's death. As a

Queen I can ensure the survival of my tribe. So, this is easy for me to make this choice. However, as a mother, to say goodbye to my children will break my heart, and only for these few moments I will allow my pain to bow my head, then we will go and tell them of my decision. A storm is coming, we must weather it as best we can."

These two traumatised women showed they were Iceni royalty, they asked just once to be allowed to stay, they cried and held their warrior mother, then turned and to Gracus said, "Take us to succour Roman."

Gracus bowed to the woman, the queen, who would in the next year wipe the 9th Legion from the pages of history and the face of the earth. Only this mission as guide and guardian to the ring keeper saved him from being with his brothers-in-arms who would be the stuff of legends in the annuls of British history forever.

Jeannie took the hand of each girl, Gracus folded her in his arms, when they opened their eyes again, the TV was still showing Murray's quarterfinal match, the Scot was looking good for another win. She switched it off as the girls faces showed sheer terror as they viewed this magic-box. Here we go again, thought Jeannie.

Twenty-one years old, a Cambridge graduate, she'd won a scholarship and had worked in the lab at the university for some time now, but she was unfulfilled. A new position promised the possibility for her to investigate some theories she harboured. In preparation and celebration of this new post in Fulham, she'd taken some rare time off. She was here, hurrying down Cambridge's Great Eastern Street, en route to Myra, her closest friend from uni. They were planning an evening with other friends in their favourite haunts before Rosalind headed into the Peak District for some rigorous hill-walking and fresh air. It was likely to be a while before she expected an opportunity to get some leave once ensconced in the 'big smoke' and her new job.

She was completely caught off guard and at a total loss moments later when the air raid sirens began their terrifying wail, heralding death and destruction from the dark night sky. The Jerries seemed to have it in for this small East Anglian town. She was not *au fait* with this area of Cambridge, her friend Myra had only moved into her new flat two days ago, having been bombed out of the lovely little terrace house in Vicarage Road that she'd inherited from her parents. Everything, photos, furniture, everything was turned to rubble and dust in a matter of moments, Rosalind hoped her friend would be able to withstand the grief she was bound to endure at such a total annihilation of her past in physical terms. Rosalind was just grateful her friend was out at the time of the raid.

She started to run, her strong legs swiftly covering ground, she hoped to spot others heading for a shelter nearby. Then, causing her to become rooted to the spot came the petrifying, screaming whistle that declared the dreaded incendiary bombs, Hitler's latest terror tactic weapon.

She was riveted and could not move her feet. Her last recollections of the moments after, would be explosions that hurt the ear, flying masonry, flames and the face of a red-haired woman and a very handsome man, in the oddest of clothes.

Jeannie woke, knowing only that Cambridge 1942 was where she needed to be, and soon. She grabbed her jeans and pulled her dirty t-shirt over her head as she ran to the spare room. Quietly opening the door and approaching the bed, she enjoyed a split second before his eyes snapped open. She drank in the sight of her legionary sprawled in the cast of a moonbeam across the bed. His muscular tanned body filled her with lustful and hungry thoughts.

"*Domina*, do you need me?"

"There is more than one answer to that question," she mused almost out loud.

Coming back to the moment, she replied, "Yes, but hurry, we need to move. Dress warm, the dreamscape was not tropical."

He was beside her on the sofa in minutes.

"Gracus, this looked like another rescue mission, but it was in a chaotic explosive moment in time. We need to be in and out in moments. So, this may be dangerous, painful and draining."

"Shall I bring the first-aid pack you showed me? Seconds may be important."

"Good idea, the woman in my vision looks fit, but injured, okay, let's go."

She smiled as he took her hand.

"Here, *Domina!*"

By his feet amongst a scattering of rubble and masonry lay the body of a woman of about twenty years or so. This attractive woman's eyelids began to flutter open accompanied by a throaty groan. Instantly the eyes filled with fear and pain. Her eyes darted every which way, no doubt in part due to the sight of Gracus in his 2017 lycra sports outfit, which revealed the ripped muscle structure and physical definitions of more than this woman was accustomed to seeing. Her appreciation was hidden quickly, but Jeannie definitely saw it in the woman's analytical eyes.

Before Rosalind could gather her wits, Gracus had cleared the debris and gathered her up into his arms, he looked up into Jeannie's face and grinned, saying, "This is a much more pleasant mission than I expected."

Jeannie's face flushed in jealous anger, "Stupid..." she muttered to herself.

"*Domina*, did you say something?" said a grinning Gracus.

"Nothing!" snapped a tongue-tied and raging Jeannie as she linked their arms to return, "and call me Jeannie!"

The three bodies dropped unceremoniously into the large, padded sofa, safe and well, if tired and sore, in the place and time Jeannie called home.

Jeannie sent Gracus for some warm water, soap, towels, and disinfectant. Whilst he was gone, the young woman sat staring around the room, she was in fight or flight mode but also, Jeannie surmised, a touch concussed and so not of a mind to panic. She had intelligent large eyes that inspected Jeannie first then her surroundings.

Satisfied in herself that Jeannie posed no immediate threat, Rosalind sat back and asked where she was, how did they get here and who was she and her husband who had so kindly assisted her? When

Gracus came back in, the anxiety was visible in the face of their guest so Jeannie asked that he go and shower and change that they might go out to eat. Whilst he did, Jeannie explained as best she could to the woman all that she needed to know, and, also asked her who she was.

"My name is Rosalind Franklin, a chemistry graduate born in London in 1920."

Gracus returned, clean shaven in a pair of dark blue jeans, a vintage button-down collared Ben Sherman shirt and casual loafers. He looked magnificent in this simple outfit. The shirt fit snuggly across his broad shoulders and muscled chest, the jeans stretched tightly round gloriously defined thigh and maximus glutinous muscles. Jeannie had to stifle the sigh that threatened to escape her, Rosalind however, could not hide her admiration. Jeannie's jealous hackles rose again, much to her annoyance, made worse by his knowing grin.

She pondered the possibility that he was aware of her growing feelings for him. She could not - would not - contemplate his thoughts on the matter. Her realisation that he'd be her guardian for life made the prospect of his rejection impossible to contemplate.

They took Rosalind to a vintage New Yorker dining experience eatery near the house in the hopes it would be more familiar than a modern place and allow her some space to relax a little. By the time they'd devoured huge cheeseburgers and fries and cheesecake Rosalind was relaxed and hungry for information about the differences between their timelines and how did the portal work, her scientific mind demanding answers they didn't have, sadly!

Later, as Jeannie sat in bed researching databases to understand who and what Rosalind would be to the world, she was saddened and surprised at what she learnt. How could the world have allowed her ground-breaking research to be buried and almost wiped from the huge leap in science that her work had facilitated? And all just because she was a woman.

She understood why they had to affect the rescue, without the woman asleep in Jeannie's guest room the fantastic work in DNA would have maybe never been discovered or at best it would have been much later in the timeline of history. Still, Jeannie hated that this woman's findings would not be lauded and accredited to her until decades after her death. Sad, she thought as she read more of this woman's bio.

Jeannie was interrupted by a quiet tap on her door. "Come in," she called.

Gracus poked his head around the door, "Did I wake you, Jeannie?"

Her heart skipped at least three beats as she realised, he had used her given name for the first time.

"No, I was swatting up on our guest. What can I do for you?"

She was unaware of the tremble in his hand, or the racing of his heart. He wasn't, and he knew this was dangerous ground, but he also knew he couldn't go on like this. It had been more than eighteen months that he'd lived under the same roof as this beautiful, funny, brave woman. His heart had been hers for more than a year, so many nights he'd found himself at her door ready to knock, only to turn and go for a run. He had run for hours trying to decide his next course of action.

He knew he would live out his life as her guardian, but he wanted more, so much more, and his heart had so much to give.

"Jeannie, I must talk to you, I cannot live like this anymore."

She grabbed a robe and got out of bed, she needed to get out of this room. She couldn't concentrate on his words, her eyes feasted on him. Loose shorts, and a vest T-shirt, they hid nothing of the glory of this one-time legionary. Once a member of the most notorious legion of the Roman empire, now her guardian. With the bed behind her she couldn't stop her mind running riot with 'what if's'.

As she tried to pass him, he said her name again, his voice husky, throaty and low, as she turned to him, he pulled her tightly to him and lowered his mouth over hers. The surprise of it caused an initial attempt to push him away, but the fierceness of his embrace and the hunger in his lips silenced any protest she might have eventually made. His long strong fingers raked her hair twisting it roughly, forcing her head back exposing her throat. She gasped, her knees threatened to buckle. He lifted his head and whispered, "*Ti amo caro.*"

she knew enough Italian to understand his declaration of love; her heart broke wide open, and he stepped straight in.

As daylight's fingers sneaked its light around the edges of her room, Jeannie sat in bed watching her guardian, her love and soon to be husband. He had not wanted to leave her but would not dishonour her by entering her bed until they had married. He had spent the night in the wingback chair by her bed. She was smiling in her tummy, the smile was infused with such joy, love, and excitement. Then she remembered Rosalind.

She crept past Gracus, barely resisting the temptation to touch him. Emerging from her room, she saw Rosalind come out of Gracus's room, she stepped into the doorframe to the lounge and allowed her guest to get passed the bathroom door which was between her room and his. She was offering up an opportunity for a lie to be spun, should her guest feel the need of one.

"Good morning Rosalind, how do you feel? I do hope you managed to sleep well for I must return you to your own time and place very soon.

"Thank you, yes, I slept well under the circumstances. It's been quite a shock."

"Were you needing something?" asked Jeannie,

"Oh yes, I was looking for Gracus, but he's not there. I could do with a long walk to clear my head and blow the cobwebs away."

Just then the doorbell rang, moments later Gracus appeared,

"Ah, just in time. Rosalind could use some fresh air, how about you take her round the lake, it's quite peaceful. Who was at the door?"

"Good morning, ladies, my pleasure *Domina*, it was the postman, my new card arrived."

Jeannie's heart sank until she spotted the glint of devilment in his eyes and the smugness of his grin, "well go on then, when you get back, we'll take you home Rosalind."

Jeannie spent the next half hour tidying up cups and dealing with washing and bed making. That's when she discovered that Gracus must have left his laptop on and open on his bed. She was about to check the history when she heard them return.

"Thank you, Jeannie, you saved my life, you and Gracus, and I will be forever grateful. "He loves you very much you know, you're a lucky woman."

Twenty minutes later, having returned Rosalind to Cambridge of 1942, Jeannie and Gracus were slumped on the sofa. "Oh, I forgot, you left your laptop on last night. I'm sorry, I should have told you about that before, but I can't always think of everything."

Laughing, as he went to go and turn it off, he kissed the top of her head then winked and grinned, "Yes, Miss," she threw the cushion at his back as he dived out the door.

He returned moments later, "Jeannie, I think Rosalind had a little look on my computer, she watched you closely when you were showing her stuff on the iPad yesterday when we brought her back here. Look."

Recent searches were all chemistry, science, and related pages, including a copy of a paper written by Rosalind Franklin on the 3D structure of DNA and her double helix images. She'd also read how Watson and Crick had 'pioneered' DNA on the back of her work without ever accrediting her with the base knowledge that opened the door for them. She knew what was coming, they wondered if she would try to change things.

Gracus sat down beside Jeannie. "Did you really agree to marry me last night?" he asked nibbling her ear. She climbed into his lap, reaching up to his mouth with hers, she replied, "Yes, I do believe I did."

"Good, so we can do it today?"

Jeannie giggled, "NO, by special licence it would be three days, and under normal posting of the banns, three weeks."

"I can't wait that long, I want forever to be able to think and say, 'she's mine."

She laughed and said, "well, you'll need to be patient."

He picked her up, putting an envelope in her hand as he made for the door, "I can use a computer too you know" he laughed,

"Destination Registry office," he whispered in her ear, she kissed his cheek, so that was what the delivery was.

"I love you Gracus Aurelius, *Mo Chridhe.*"

Part Five: It Was a Very Special Day

Jeannie had discussed exactly how things were to proceed if they found Alfred where history reported him to have been at the time of the battle.

Gracus tended to believe the rumour that Ubba, the most fearsome of the three brothers who were delaying Alfred's plans to create Engleland, had in fact been killed by the King himself and not by Odda of Devon.

It was now as natural as brushing one's hair to step into the time void. Fifteen years had flown by since Jeannie had first learnt of her great-aunt's bequest and had embarked on this fantastical journey. A journey that had led her to Gracus, the ring bearer's guardian. Her soulmate, the love of her life and now, too, her husband. Gracus Aurileus, a Roman centurion and father of her two children, Cornelia and Marcus. Her great-aunt's bequest mayhap, had led her to an unusual life, but one full of love and happiness. Oh, and adventure.

Now, the ring, after a period of inactivity called to her to return to the year of our Lord, 878 and the great battle of Cynwit, in what is now the county of Devon, England. King Alfred the Great's life was in danger....

Jeannie stepped into Gracus's arms and spoke the now familiar words, and in the blink of an eye, they found themselves on the approach to Countisbury Hill with the lights of the Inn up ahead and the chapel behind them. The had procured re-enactors outfits suitable for the period to avoid calling any more attention upon them than just being strangers to the area might bring.

Jeannie's worry that history's vagueness as to the true location of this battle might prove a problem: However, she'd learnt to trust in the ring. So here she and her centurion husband stood, awaiting the arrival of Alfred and Ubba's forces. She knew that the Viking warrior would bring a force of twelve-hundred battle-hardened warriors to the field, history gave no account of Odda's numbers.

Dawn broke over the beautiful, rugged coastline, an orange light giving the sea an illusion of being covered with a liquid fire, glittering, changing, and dancing with the movement of the waves. It was an image Jeannie would have loved to have captured on her camera, which of course lay in her drawer back home, more than 1,000 years in the future.

To their right on the high ground, Gracus spotted the banners of the Devon Yeomanry, at their head, the great red banner with the golden dragon of the King of Wessex, Alfred! The plan to remove themselves should historians prove correct in their claim that Alfred was in Chippenham at his Court, was now obsolete, if history was to continue as it is written, they had important work to do.

Odda held his men, as instructed by Alfred, on the high ground. This meant Jeannie and Gracus had to approach from behind to avoid being mistaken for Danes. This took longer than they'd hoped, and it was nearing mid-day by the time they sauntered through the camp.

Gracus begged to be allowed to just grab the King and meet Jeannie behind his horse lines. Jeannie favoured a discussion, in the hopes of persuasion. However, fate took a hand in the proceedings as they approached the Royal standard that identified Alfred's tent. They could hear Odda's voice raised in a passionate argument, pleading to be permitted to lead the men down to attack whilst they might still have the element of surprise. Alfred dismissed Odda, saying he felt unwell and would rest and consider all possible plans.

This was their only hope, their one chance....

Gracus and Jeannie feigned being lovers and headed into the shrubbery behind the royal tent, once out of sight, Gracus used his *gladius* to rent the tents rear panel open from top to bottom, and before Alfred had a chance to call out, had disabled and silenced this great leader of men.

Jeannie asked if Alfred would grant them an audience and gleaned his promise not to call his guards until they had explained their reasons for such audacious actions upon His Majesty. It was their claim that it concerned his plans to create the kingdom of Engleland that swayed him. Gracus was certain that at this point in time, Alfred had not made this plan and his proposed name for his unification of the many kingdoms public outside a trusted few.

Alfred appraised the two, and demonstrating the wisdom he became famous for, agreed to hear these two strangers, who although spoke the language of his kingdom, did so with an unknown accent. He had an agenda in this too, he wanted to know the traitor in his court that knew and spoke of his secret plans for his country.

Jeannie put forward the argument to allow Odda to carry out his plan, and Alfred should remove himself from the field and return to his court.

Having given his word, Gracus had removed his hand from Alfred's mouth. In a soft yet authoritative voice

Alfred refused to allow himself to be seen running away from the battlefield.

Jeannie was considering her next move when there was heard a cry from outside declaring the Vikings had arrived. Twenty- three ships were pulling onto the beaches and spilling over the sides were in excess of one thousand battle hardened fighting men. The Danes soon took up positions that cut off any access to the fresh water. This now changed things dramatically. Odda had to be allowed to act.

Suddenly three huge Vikings burst through the back of the tent, obviously sent with orders to assassinate Arthur to demoralise the Saxon forces, thereby winning the day possibly without a fight.

They had not accounted for Gracus, the sole survivor of the famous Ninth Legion of Rome, who proved more than a match for these wild men who were taken by surprise. As the last man fell, Jeannie called Gracus to her, and each taking an arm, held Arthur the King in a group hug as she uttered the ancient chant that spun them out of the place of Ubba's demise.

There had been no other choices left for her, but they didn't travel too far, they came to themselves on the road to Chippenham, it was still before the noonday bell on whatever day this was. They escorted Alfred to the entrance to the town, bidding him farewell, they disappeared, their final words echoing in Alfred's ears, "Don't give up."

Gracus landed on the sofa first, Jeannie dropping into his lap a second later.

"Wow that was so cool, to save Alfred the Great and England, that's a very special day."

Gracus pulled her into his arms, silencing her with his mouth, "Shh! you'll wake the kids!"

Graphic by Eduardo Davad, from Pixabay

Embezzlement

Catriona looked over at her tall, athletic, handsome and very sexy looking husband, he looked past her, she turned to see his Capo enter, he smiled at her. (Seducing him had been so easy).

As the No 1 Capo in the family business, he was in charge of security and accounts for the Don's family as well as the business. Although it was a small group it was very lucrative.

Set just on the edge of Silicon Valley, their home sat on the coast west of the Sam Francisco Bay, above a small town with the lovely name of Half Moon Bay. Their place was a Spanish built house in its own gated community. Money had been no object to decorate and furnish. It was now a stunning yet comfortable home.

Sounds like paradise doesn't it? How wrong you'd be.

She'd met and married Nico Martinelli in Edinburgh where they'd attended university. He was taking business and economics and she art and history. He'd literally swept her off her feet. She'd been standing chatting with her closest friend, Aileen, when suddenly she was scooped upt off the ground by a pair of strong arms attached to the face and body of a Latin God.

Within six months they'd married, Nico said he was studying to take over the family business in "the Valley…" California. His parents had flown in for the quiet wedding in the beautiful Catholic cathedral of St Mary's which faces the top of Leith walk.

Catriona had worshipped there often as a wee girl with her father. Wonderful Sunday mornings of mass then going to the to the BBQ, a very modern American style diner for burgers and ice cream sodas, with her father, and hero.

They had worked hard, and the five years of study, and work experience in some high-flying accounts firm for Nico and the Museum of Antiquities for her, meant their life was wonderful, loving and fulfilled.

In the spring of their sixth year, she was astonished to discover she was pregnant as she had been so very careful. Although Nico was more eager than she to start a family, he'd understood that she wanted to wait and achieve some advancement within her profession first. After the initial shock and seeing the raw joy in

Nico's face when she'd told him, she'd caved and threw herself into the preparations for the birth of their first child. Just about four months in, after the first trimester worry time had passed, Nico announced he'd been called back home. Obviously, his parents wanted their son and his family near as they approached retirement.

Reluctantly Catriona said good bye to her beloved homeland. Her parents having passed some years before and Aileen now was working and living in London. It sounds like an easy choice, but it wasn't, Scotland was her home.

Two miscarriages and three years later, she'd found herself in an impossible to comprehend situation. The family business was not the computer chip industry as she'd assumed, but *La Cosa Nostra*, (Our Affair), The Mafia. Her once loving husband, now cold, and disappointed by their lack of children, was now the Don. A leader of drug dealers, pimps, and killers. Hardest to bear was the knowledge that he kept a mistress, whom she'd discovered three years ago. This woman had been delivered of a child… Nico's!

When his son was about six months old, he'd announced that Sophia and Alfredo would be moving into the compound. Draped and paraded under her nose. This was the step too far.

She vowed to leave him, but Nico had made it perfectly clear this was not an option; as Catholics, no attempt at divorce could even be discussed. The same went for separation, he refused to consider it.

Catriona had never responded well to being ordered about.

Roberto was Nico's capo, his right-hand man. His father had insisted, Roberto was the son of his father's mistress, he was raised within the compound just as Nico planned for 'Fredo.

She'd seen the way the capo watched her and noted how solicitous he was.

The plan had come to her after an accident, she'd slipped and fallen on the steps to the terrace and badly broken her leg. Nico had assigned Robbie, as she called him, to take her to the hospital in San Jose, he'd been so sweet with her.

After two hours waiting for the x ray results and three days as a patient who'd had surgery to set the bones with pins, they were comfortably relaxed in each-others company and had shared much of their life history.

By the time she was discharged, two things had cemented her decision to act. The first was, Nico never once came to see her, he hadn't called her direct to ask after her wellbeing, not even a bunch of flowers. The second, Roberto had let it slip that he and Nico disliked each other intensely and it was only their father and the *Cosa Nostra* law that forced them to be civil and work together. There may have been some self-preservation in there too, as their lives depended upon the certainty that each would do their jobs, for the "Family"

She had encouraged their friendship, careful to not let Nico see anything but a cool distain for his capo. Nico's attitude towards her was, providing that she did nothing to shame the family or himself, she was permitted relative freedom.

Roberto feigned resistance at being delegated to babysit his boss's wife.

As I said before, Catriona encountered little resistance from Roberto. So, after two years of flirting, innuendo and unadulterated flattery, she fabricated a need to visit San Francisco, to advise on an artefact from the historic era which was the niche she specialised in. Aileen had agreed during a long conversation on the throwaway mobile that Catriona had bought at the mall. She used it but twice and then threw away. It had been agreed that Aileen would write to her from the London gallery asking her to do a courtesy for one of her clients who'd requested this meeting. It was arranged in the letter that the so-called client would call her with dates and venue in 'Frisco. Aileen's partner Jake would in fact be the caller.

Nico was against it of course, but in the middle of the heated row, she'd thrown down a gauntlet. Not only was she going, but the wolfhound gaoler wasn't going with her either. (here was the deal breaker, she banked on Nico's reply), he bit, hook line and sinker, yelling,

"You're going nowhere without him so he most definitely is going with you."

"No, no, no! " she yelled to force them past the not going stage.

He screamed, "Do not defy me, Catriona!" slamming the door as he left.

He missed the slow smile and fist punch. She'd got exactly what she wanted. So predictable... A dangerous trait for a Don she mused as she entered her study to draw together the strings of her plan.

Two weeks in 'Frisco was wonderful, she toyed with Robbie, luring him further into her tender trap. She slammed the door on his final chance to escape when she pretended to faint in the elevator as Robbie escorted her to her room on the final night of their trip.

He had spent the whole of the day, declaring his devotion and slating Nico for a fool who didn't know the value of the woman he'd married. Almost every evening of their two weeks he'd promised her the earth, the moon and the stars if she could reciprocate just a fraction of his feelings for her.

As predictable as his half- brother, she knew Robbie was cool, calm and decisive in an emergency, so when she slid down the side of the elevator car in a faint, he'd just scooped her up and strode the corridor to her room. Ordering the bus boy to get the key from her purse, to open the door and turn on the lights. Roberto laid her on the huge luxurious bed and returned to the door, he tipped the boy well and tapping the side of his nose, he winked at the lad as he closed the suite door.

Roberto got a flannel and steeped it in cold water, he returned with the wrung out cold cloth for her forehead. Her eyes fluttered open, she hoped she'd framed her expression exactly to show some confusion and a glint of fear. Robbie saw exactly what she'd wanted him to. She began to weep, she whispered,

"Sorry Robbie, I thought I was coming out from another attack from Nico."

Roberto's face was a mask of incandescent rage for about 30 seconds, then he threw caution to the wind, put his hand gently behind her neck and pulled her into his arms and kissed her. Just as she'd planned.

Before dawn broke they had formulated their plan of escape. Robbie would divert a small amount from every "enterprise" the family were involved with. It would go into an offshore account in the name of Roma Lucas. The names were the names she'd silently given to the children she'd delivered, a daughter and a son that had drawn breath for less than an hour each. Within two years, Roma Lucas had become a very rich woman.

Sitting in the breakfast room with both her husband and her lover, Catriona stopped to ponder. How, in God's name, had she come to this, those loving, happy years with Nico seemed like they'd happened to two different people.

Robbie it turned out was so like Nico. Ruthless when he felt it needed.

He'd arranged the death of one of his soldiers, the man had spotted a letter on Roberto's desk addressed to Roma Lucas, the fool had asked who she was, saying with a lewd gesture, "A bit on the down low eh Capo."

The same night, to minimise the chance that the inquisitive fool had mentioned it to anyone other than his family, Roberto had paid an outside contractor to ensure an accident wiped out the whole family. He had told her, expecting her to be impressed by the lengths he was willing to go to protect them. She wasn't in need of protection.

She knew there was nothing to tie her to the account or the theft. She'd always been cool and occasionally belligerent towards Robbie; their affair was a well-hidden secret.

She pulled herself from her reverie and moved to detonate the final part of her plan. She knew exactly how Nico would react if he knew any part of Roberto's betrayal. He would not tolerate his actions against "the Family" or himself personally. She gave a sly smile to Robbie as he left.

Nico believed Robbie was off to a meeting with a local drug lord. He was in fact heading to the airport after stopping at the bank to withdraw a third of the total in the account. They had decided that this amount of cash would be enough to get them away and "lost" long enough to create a new identity with no paper trail at all. The rest was to sit and be there until they'd created a safe new life. She of course had the card and the PIN in case of any unforeseen eventualities. A letter had been lodged with a man who owed Roberto his life, stating Catriona had Power of Attorney and was to be given assistance in any request she made, providing she was alone when she tried to access the account. It was just a precaution she said, in case they had to change plans on the fly.

Five minutes later she casually asked Nico, "Do you trust Robbie?"

Confusion flickered over his face, he replied, "Of course," he growled.

She laughed; as she did, Nico grabbed her jaw in a vice like grip. "What is wrong with you, woman?" he snarled.

She smiled saying, "Nothing, but I didn't realise how much you had changed. Not only are you an adulterer, a cruel and cold husband, but now you are also a blind fool. I am leaving you for Robbie, and you didn't see it coming... some Don..."

His hand shot out and the punch caught her hard and she went down, and as planned, she stayed down. He was too angry to care if she was out cold or dead, he was out of the front door calling all his men to him.

Catriona waited until she heard the car doors slam and all the cars screech away. After a minute or two she could tell the house was empty. She moved like an athlete, into the hall, grabbed her bag and walked to the gates, it was not unusual for the guards there to see her with a red welt on her cheek and she'd often go for a walk to calm down after a row. They let her pass without looking her in the eye.

She took the first right, pulled a set of keys from her bag, and got into the black nondescript saloon she'd bought for this short trip. She walked into the bank in San Jose; it had taken just shy of an hour from Half Moon Bay to the bank. Now she was leaving, the money transferred to an account with a Swiss bank who were renowned for their privacy policy.

Catriona had been busy over the last two years: she'd changed her name in the UK by deed declaration online and sent the documents via email to Aileen, who opened a Royal Bank of Scotland account in the new name. The total sum in the account she jointly held with Roberto had been transferred to the Swiss bank then immediately to the RBS account.

Aileen had hired a private plane to meet Catriona on the tarmac at Howard Airfield. It was just over two hours away, but Mineta International Airport would be where Roberto would be, and soon enough so too Nico and his men.

She made good time and within the course of a morning, she'd done it. Freedom!

Nico would want his revenge, but his position as Don would have been undermined by Roberto's betrayal and embezzlement, the bigger families would have something to say about this. She figured it would be years before he'd be out from under the Sicilian big guns enough to try to come after her.

In the end, she didn't have to worry at all, it was all over the news:

Five Die in Mineta Airport Shootout

San Jose. *It is believed that Don Martinelli had discovered his Capo and half- brother Roberto Martinelli had been embezzling from the "family business," He'd caught up with his sibling at the airport just about to go through to departures.*

He carried a ticket for the Bahamas in his pocket. According to police sources a gun was pulled and a firefight erupted between the Don, the Capo and airport police. It is yet to be confirmed but it seems Nico's shot killed his brother and police shot Don Martinelli and one other of his thugs. One local police officer was also killed.

Catriona sent a large anonymous cheque to the police officer's family, no true compensation for a loved one, but it would help ease the life they had to live without him.

Catriona is now living and working as a psychotherapist in a small highland town in Scotland. She has one wonderful, unexpected gift from her past life, a daughter she delivered eight and a half months after her escape. Roma Roberta is a delight to both her and Roma's favourite aunty, Aileen.

Silhouette

Her fiancé, her parents, her brothers, and friends all knew it was a long road that lay ahead for Neave. Recovery would be fought for with blood, sweat and tears.

Neave had been on her way to Warrington Academy, hoping to secure a new job and the beginning of her dreams on the work front. She was walking down Bridge Street, a main thoroughfare like many high streets across the country. One moment trying to avoid collision with two boys chasing each other in the way of boys aged about eleven or twelve. The next, all she could recall, was a deafening noise, pain... then nothing.

Nothing was all she could recall prior to the image of the two boys laughing and chasing each other. She regained consciousness weeks later after two operations, one on her spine, the other on her skull. She'd seen images on the TV of the casualties, one, a twelve-year-old boy. One of the faces that was almost the sum total of her memory. Regaining the use of her legs was going to take time and prayers.

Sean, her fiancé, had flown down from Glasgow with her parents, Charlie and Vi. He'd come from their home in Coatbridge, a small village on the outskirts of the city. Her parents had driven to Glasgow from Milton of Buchanan, a hamlet near Balmaha on the shores of Loch Lomond.

Sean knew the inactivity would be Neave's Achilles heel in her recovery process. They usually spent their weekends, potholing, walking the glens or climbing the Munros all over the highlands. Their favourite place though was round Loch Lomond, and so often could be found at her parent's old school house home in Milton. The Winnock in Drymen was a favourite watering hole, especially on *ceilidh* nights when the *craic* was fierce.

He worried at how they'd manage to help her regain her physical health, but he was terrified she'd never regain her memories, memories of their life and love. He couldn't bear the idea he might lose her…

Meanwhile, their families and friends fought the rage they felt towards the terrorists who'd planted the bomb that had injured their girl.

Neave sat staring out the window of the ward in the Manchester hospital where she'd been since the bombing. She was waiting to be transferred to Queen Elizabeth's Spinal unit in the centre of Glasgow. She'd understood the need for the transfer. The excellence of this pioneering unit and the nearness to her home, family and friends -- all of which might be helpful for the retrieval of her memory.

It made sense to everyone, except Neave... Neave! Even her name sounded alien to her ears. The one glimmer of something akin to hope, happened when the man called Sean had fallen asleep propped on her pillows, her head on his shoulder. In a split second before total consciousness, she realised that while her mind had forgotten him, her body had not.

She'd had barely a moment to register the physical recognition of the body or presence of a man she'd loved for years. She knew this man and they had been close, she had to trust her instincts. She would allow him to be himself with her, as if she knew him. She felt he represented hope, and that was all she had.

They'd been working hard in the physio department with her, but she'd begun to get caustic, uncooperative and acerbic. Sean knew that the weeks of being caged and being without the wind in her hair or the sun on her face was making her stir-crazy. He fought hard with the consultants, and Charlie and Vi had backed him up, they knew their daughter and how she loved and thrived in the outdoors. The smell of the heather and broom, the sounds of the peewit on the moors and the rugged hills and glens were like water and air for their tomboy daughter. If anything could lift her, it was to get out for a while.

Under serious orders and promises procured that there'd be no rough tracks or long periods on her sticks, finally, her doctors agreed. Sean knew exactly where they would go.

First, they were going to her Mum and Dad in Milton, they'd lunch on the decking, watching the river running below, and just enjoy the people and the place so familiar to them.

Vi had made Neave's favourite - stovies and Forfar bridie - which has to be said, she ate with relish, even commenting that these were the best tastes ever, everyone laughed. Sean saw a momentary startled look flicker over her face and hoped the food, love and relaxed atmosphere, had prodded her memory a little. One glass of Prosecco was all she'd been told she could have, and she enjoyed that too, declaring she'd have another go at another bottle of that brand at a later date.

When lunch was over and finally cleared away, Sean got the open-topped jeep out of the garage and brought it right up to the door. Gently, he lifted her from the wheelchair up into the passenger seat, pretending as he'd often done when whisking her off her feet, that he was too weak to carry her weight. She laughed, and without pause, reacted as she always had, swatting his butt whilst kissing his cheek. He laughed, again he spotted a flicker of something pass across her eyes.

He drove up to Balmaha and pulled into the carpark at the visitor's centre, going to the very spot where last year he'd proposed to her. He parked up and lifted her down into the wheelchair. As they rounded the corner of the building, the grey sky and even darker grey of the loch, created a soulful silhouette of the lone tree, *their tree*, at the water's edge. An iconic image, moody or joyous, depending on the weather and light.

He pushed the chair to the path's edge where the tree stood and bent to put the brakes on. As he looked up into the face of his childhood sweetheart, tears were rolling down her cheeks and a sob wracked her body before it rose into a primal howl, at which point, Neave threw herself into his arms.

"I remember you, oh Sean, how did I ever forget who you are to me?"

"Shh, baby," he whispered, "you remember now, that's all that matters. Out of curiosity, what was it that pushed passed the fog wall?"

"Our tree, the silhouette of it against the water is exactly how it was the day you first brought me here and we shared our first kiss. I was fifteen, you just turned seventeen. The image of that tree marks so many milestones in our life. I told it all my secrets as a child too, so all my memories were here waiting."

The Tiger

The boy, Raj, played against the back of his home. The bamboo and mud of the rear wall was a perfect place to practice his over-arm spin. The impact left a dust mark, so he could check his accuracy. His parents smiled indulgently upon their seven-year old son. His declared intent, being the best bowler India had ever had, warmed their heart. His enthusiasm was infectious, but his mother knew too, that his dream was impossible. The caste system would never allow a Dalit - an untouchable - to attain such stature in any field.

His life would be hard, forced to earn a living doing the most menial of jobs, the dirtiest jobs going. Or he could stay and farm on the edge of Assam where it borders with Bhutan. Bhutan means highlands, and it was well named, being in the valleys and peaks of the Himalayas. His mother often cried at night asking Brahma why she'd been cursed to be born in the lowest caste, sentencing for all eternity her children to lives of poverty, enriched only by the love of their mother and the toil of their father.

Raj's father wished he could assure his wife that he had a plan, but he was afraid to speak of it for fear he'd curse it. He intended to breed his goat, and every kid she had would be sold and put into a fund. When Raj was 15, it was his father's dream to send him to his uncle in England. There he could play his glorious game and maybe, maybe then he could achieve his dream.

Raj was seven, and since almost the entire village were of the same caste, he was blissfully happy and totally unaware of the precarious nature of his dreams, and the probable disappointment that awaited him.

Today he was practicing becoming the next Vinoo Mankand, who in the 1951/52 test series, had almost single-handedly been responsible for the resounding victory that gave India her first test win. Tales of Vinoo's prowess travelled the length and breadth of India and indeed the world. Raj had an uncle who worked in Haldwani in Uttarakland, and he had seen Vinoo in his welcome-home parade after that glorious series. He brought photos and newspaper cuttings to Raj when he came back to visit his mother, Raj's much loved Nani, who lived with him and his parents.

When he focused on his cricketing prowess, Raj was oblivious to all, and was a happy boy.

Bagha was tired, he'd been chased from the higher villages in what people would call Nepal. He had been scavenging on the edges of a village and had been lying in the sun when he saw one of the human young, fall from a high wall. She lay there for a long time and as the sun began to dip, he moved closer.

He had killed enough prey to recognise death, and whilst ordinarily he would have preferred to eat after the pleasure of the hunt, only a fool turns from a free meal. It was still warm, and it had been a long time since his last feast. He had barely broken the skin on the plump leg when he was caught unawares by a large group of men with sticks. They had him with his back to the wall as they formed a semi-circle hemming him in. He picked up his meal and tried to charge through to freedom. He made his escape but not before he'd taken several hard blows from the heavy wooden sticks.

Bagha raced without thought of anything except the pain in his right shoulder and freedom. Hunger had instigated his first mistake, panic and pain caused his second and almost fatal error. He ran exactly where he was meant to and missed the sticks and foliage covering the pit. One huge bound found him land on shifting ground and into the deep pit he fell. He knew he was seriously hurt. The race had been intensely painful, exacerbated now by an awkward landing in the pit. They left him there to die, taking the child's body with them. He didn't understand their anger, he had not killed the child.

That he lived was an accident, he didn't know what animal or group of animals had passed one night, he was quite weak as he'd been in the heat for days without water as well as food. Whatever it was that passed, their movements had shifted some of the branches and they fell into his tomb like a ladder out of hades. He had only enough strength to drag himself out, much later in the day he crawled towards the sound of water. There he drank, and in the cave nearby, he rested for many days.

He was able to walk but his shoulder had not healed well, he knew he'd never down a water buffalo, a deer or even a boar would out-run him like this. His stealth was unimpaired, but speed was vital in the hunt, he was doomed to starve after all.

He had travelled for many days when he heard noise, a repetitive noise, an irritating noise, then he heard a voice, a female voice, calling, repetitively, also irritating. He saw some huts, and oh, praise be to the God of all, there was a goat. Tied to the tree near one of the huts. Maybe he'd survive a little longer. Maybe the food would give him strength and he'd heal. It was getting towards dusk, soon he would eat.

Raj was in charge of feeding the goat and for milking her. It was his first and his last chore of the day. Tonight, because of his practice and devious delaying before dinner, he was now later than usual. It was his habit to milk Bakara before his meal, then he and his father would play *Moksha Patam*, (snakes and ladders) until it was time for him to sleep.

He wanted it done quickly in case his father decided not to play and went to the meeting place, where the men played cards and drank coffee.

Bakara stood patiently, she dreamt of having a kid, so her milk went to her kind and not the humans, even if they did treat her well.

He had just bent to reach for Bakara's teat when Bagha struck. Raj saw his future disappear in the reflection of the huge tiger's eyes.

Bagha was happy as he gorged in the late evening sun. He was so busy eating he didn't notice the man at the window of the hut, nor did he hear the loud "crack!" of the shot. He died instantly. Raj's father held his old Lee-Enfield army rifle, he never missed then, and he didn't now.

More than one dream died that evening... but which ones?

The Break

The break happened quietly, without fuss or drama, just a bump from a felled giant fir. But, like the boxer with the glass jaw, the biggest can be felled, and it doesn't take much effort if hit directly on the weak and fragile fault. This unassuming tree had done exactly that at four a.m., on the Wednesday morning. Two days later, the barrier hit by the tree would be gone, and the tree one hundred miles to the south.

Jorgen Sigfridsson was the dam's manager, a short, fat, lazy man who rarely descended the long winding stairs or travelled in the cage lift to the galleries below. The places below the water level, where close inspections should be made and logged regularly. Instead, he left this laborious work to his juniors, who - under his tutelage - had not been properly instructed or assigned the job. Consequently, they only viewed these areas occasionally and then only in passing.

Leif Eriksson was snoozing in the office chair on level twenty, about thirty meters below water level on the near side when he heard a distinct cracking sound.

He immediately called to the office of Mr Sigfridsson, "Sir, I think there's a problem."

"What kind of problem?" replied his boss distractedly. Mr Sigfridsson was watching X-rated videos on his laptop and barely listening.

"Sir, I heard a loud crack."

"Settlement noises or your vivid imaginings, there's no warning lights on is there?"

Leif was buckling, "No, sir, but it was loud."

Almost like an absent-minded professor his boss then said, "OK, so go and look, and don't call me back unless there's something to report."

Leif was beginning to feel embarrassed at his panicked call, but he had heard the crack, so he set off to walk the 800 meters of gallery on this level. An hour later having traversed the full width of the structure, almost a mile of metal walkways and concrete, he was back at his post. Feeling decidedly stupid, "I have behaved like a spooked rookie" he chided himself.

Hence, later, much later when he heard another louder crack, he didn't log that nor call his boss. He didn't want to be seen as gullible or scared. Though he knew in his heart he was.

He was very relieved when his shift ended. It was the longest twelve-hour shift experience in his six months on the job. He signed out of the daily log and headed for the cage lift that would carry him topside. Arriving at the viewing platform and admin offices he blinked in the bright sunshine.

It had been twenty-nine hours since the fir tree had so gently nudged the dam.

Ragnar Havard signed in to work at 0845 hrs. As he was taking over from Leif, they chatted, "Anything I need to know?" Ragnar asked.

Leif momentarily considered telling Ragnar about the cracking sounds but bottled it, "Nope, all good my friend. Are you coming to the bar tonight Ragnar?"

Ragnar didn't particularly like Leif, but crews who worked the dam had to rely on each other, so he replied

"Yes, OK, I'll see you there, but it will be later I've errands to run first."

Leif waved as he went through the door saying, "Don't be too late, you'll miss all the fun."

Ragnar headed to the cage and descended to his post on Level 20. He did cursory checks on switches, and he included some metallurgical tests on the girders and walkways. He must remember to look at damp and condensation levels.

All in all, there were quite few tasks, and he was busy for the first couple of hours. Everything seemed as it should be except for a moisture reading, it was up by 0.5. He called his boss, "Mr Sigfridsson, the moisture level is up half of a point."

"Ok, check it again," Jorgen looked at his watch, it was 13:39 hrs, "check it again at 16:00 hrs and let me know the results, okay?"

"Yes sir." the line clicked and went dead, Sigfridsson had hung up!

At 15:41 hrs Ragnar was walking the gallery heading back to his post to report again to his boss. He'd finally finished the check on the whole 800 meters when he heard an almighty noise. A noise that made his sphincter clench and his blood chill. He knew, his gut knew, long seconds before his brain acknowledged and processed it into words.

He took off like a rocket heading for the midway cage to access topside. He threw himself into the cage, his heart almost exploding from his chest, he slammed the button that would take him from this tomb. He knew if he didn't get out fast, this would be his grave.

So, so slowly it seemed that the cage climbed, 19, 18, 17, up it went, he was sure his heart would burst it was beating so fast. 9, 8, 7…

"Come on… come on!" He grabbed the phone, he didn't wait to identify who answered, he just blurted out, "Tell the boss I'm coming up. Get everyone off the dam." He looked up, 4, 3, then in that moment, the same moment he heard Sigfridsson say, "Don't be a damned idiot."

He heard the other sound; the unmistakeable sound of rushing water, crashing concrete and twisting steel. The cage went dark. Power was gone. He then heard a strange snapping sound. Just as his mind identified it, the gate bucked before beginning its furious freefall descent. Ragnar screamed, but no-one heard.

The newspapers, TV, all the media were full of the horrifying toll this disaster had visited upon the area. A village lower down the fjord was destroyed and hundreds were missing.

Almost 100 miles away a logger hauled a huge fir from the water. He'd never know it was this tree that was the catalyst to the disaster. He went about his work: he had many crosses to make for the burials upriver.

The Lochend Murder

Detective Inspector Munro entered the flat door on the left side of the stair. Typical of the four-unit blocks built by Edinburgh Corporation before WW II. There are two flats at ground level either side of the main stairs leading to the two upper homes, whose doors were left and right at the top of the stair. He knew them well. He'd once lived in the next stair. He'd been chums with the sons of the deceased. They'd been in the same queue the day he joined up in the early forties.

Going in, the bathroom was to the right, the smaller bedroom to the left, midway on the right was the coal bunker, essentially a cupboard part boarded to waist level where the coalman would empty the hundredweight of coal. At the end of the passage another door led into the living room. Immediately to the left was a large bedroom then over on the far right, past the fireplace, was the door to the scullery. Not a massive home, but it was more than enough for a family of five in the nineteen twenties.

James Munro was the son of a carriage and wagons examiner with the railways, a wheeltapper. Hence there was no judgement, only nostalgia, as he moved through his old neighbour's home.

Kitty had been found by her eldest son on his daily visit with the paper and vanilla cakes and her favourite, a meringue. The cakebox sat on the table untouched. Kitty's body was facing into the scullery, one slipper lay adrift at the foot of her chair nearby and there was blood on the fender surround of the fireplace.

"A tragic accident, there's a patch of worn carpet, looks like she caught her slipper, and the fender did the deed to her skull."

Sergeant Campbell looked sadly at the wee woman of about 50 or so who lay crumpled on the floor before him. "Aye Tam, ye might think so if you didn't know her," said Detective Munro.

He paused and bent, took her chin gently in his thumb and middle finger and moved it up and down. "Well now, either rigor has been and gone or not yet had time to manifest. Danny found his mother at eleven thirty or there abouts, so, she's either been gone since between 04:10 hrs the day, or since yesterday about the same time."

"How's that, sir?"

"Rigor sets in within one and six hours after death, it can last up to eighteen hours, so work it out Tam. Mind the coroner will give us a more accurate fix on T.O.D. once he gets her to the morgue. But one thing I do know for sure, this was no accident."

Just then, the lads from the pathology lab arrived and with gentle care removed the deceased woman's body.

Detective Munro asked for door-to-door inquiries, "Anything out of the ordinary, a face that didnae fit, a stranger? Someone may have seen something."

Jim paused in his writing of the initial report, he allowed his gaze to wander across the rooftops of Portobello houses to the Firth of Forth. White cotton-wool clouds scudded across the horizon, high above the huge container ship leaving Leith docks. It was heading out into the fierce, cold, North Sea. Bass Rock was part hidden in a sea mist, he loved this view, he always had, even as a bairn.

So far, he'd been updated that nothing yet had come from the door-to-door inquiries. He lifted the large shortbread tin that had been Kitty's. Opening it he found the usual; two penny insurances from the 20s - no fortunes there - another more recent, but again it would barely pay for the wake and the funeral. He pondered over the small savings sum, thinking of her life, her sons. Judging from these papers, he felt he could rule the boys out of his list of suspects. At least she wasn't killed for the contents of her will.

Danny, her eldest was a real gentleman in every sense of the word: a scholar, now a teacher. Tommy - her middle son - had moved to a lovely wee village outside the city. The kind you find in any direction out of Auld Reekie. Tommy was a family man and, like his older brother, doted on his Mammy.

Their father had returned from the carnage of WW I, but lived only another ten years... ten hard, cold and violent years. He left Kitty with three boys, aged two, four, and six. She had scrubbed floors, taken in washing and many other jobs to ensure her boys didn't go cold or hungry.

Alex, the youngest, had been a sickly child from birth and ended up a proper 'mummy's boy'. Now grown, he was a gambler and a drinker, and never held a job for very long. Yet Jim knew in his gut that Alex couldn't have done this either. He turned up at the house later, having spent the night at a woman's flat down off Easter Road.

Scene-Of-Crime Officers were now done and had called to say they were examining some small finds from the house and would keep him informed.

"Can we remove the police tape now, sir, we're getting an earache off the neighbour as she cannae get into the back green with the stairs and back door being taped off?"

"Aye Constable, woe betide a man that gets in the way of a wee wifey and her Monday wash." He chuckled and returned to the contents of the box.

Oh, now this is interesting he thought. He was looking at a pile of birth, marriage, and death certificates. One had instantly caught his eye, a death certificate for a wee baby girl, born in nineteen thirty-six, died aged just three months. Poor Kitty. The really interesting thing though, was the dates, born twelve years ago, six years after she was widowed.

Maybe it's nothing, the father's name was not on the certificate, but it wasn't required for a death, but usually was included. Definitely worth a chase-up.

A little later he entered the Records Office. It always felt like a library to him, everyone moving quietly and no chattering between the tables as folk researched and searched the threads of their family trees. Uncovering long lost relatives – or heart-shattering secrets.

Jeannie Watt worked here, and they had collaborated before.

"Jeannie, hello, how are you keeping?"

"Hello detective, I'm fine thanks, enjoying this fine weather for a change. What can I do for you today?"

"I need some help. Can you see what you can find relating to this death, and anything relating to this family that might raise a question or an eyebrow? It's important."

"Aye, leave it with me and I'll get back to you at the station tomorrow."

Jim thanked her and left, heading to the car and back to the station. His Sergeant and driver – Tam - had news for him as he climbed into the comfy seats of the Wolsey.

"Sir, the station has been on the radio, the autopsy and cause of death reports are on your desk."

"Righto, back to the shop, via Giovani's on the Broadway. Something tells me this is going to be a very, long day, and I've missed lunch and breakfast already."

"Giovani's it is, sir."

The smell of chips slathered in salt and sauce caused him to salivate, and he made short work of the poke of chips wrapped in last night's pink news. "Sometimes, a poke o' chips just really hits the spot, know what I mean Tam?"

"I do, sir, wish I'd got myself some now." They both laughed and alighted the car.

Jim sat at his desk and reached for the envelope from the coroner's office. As he pulled the sheets from the A4 envelope he noted the time of death was fixed between ten and eleven the previous night. He read on: death was caused by a blow to the head, the fender was all sharp angles. The report stated a smooth rounded object would be consistent with the wound. "No accidental fall to the fender, then…" he mused.

Just then, there was a knock on his door and Tam entered, he had a similar envelope in his hand, "Here's S.O.C.O's report sir, and Jeannie Watt has been on the blower, she's holding on line three for you, sir."

"Thanks Tam," he said reaching for the phone. About ten minutes later he replaced the receiver, grabbed his sports jacket, and headed for the door.

"Get the car, Tam, were off to Morningside so don't forget your cap lad, the toffs are a pernickety lot sometimes."

They pulled up outside a double-fronted Victorian house on Napier Road. The large front-gated garden sported laburnum, rhododendrons, and a profusion of wonderfully scented roses, creating a beautiful vista.

He pulled the large brass bellpull. Moments later a man in his early to mid-sixties appeared.

"Can I help you?" he asked, smiling.

"Are you Jack Fernie, previously of Duddingston Mews?"

"And you are whom?" came the rather supercilious reply.

"My apologies, sir, I am Detective Inspector James Munro, Midlothian Police."

"And what can I help you with Detective?"

"Might we come in, sir, we've some questions relating to the death of someone you might know?"

"Very well, come through to my study."

He paused before following us in, "Mabel, could you bring some tea and an extra cup to my study please, we have visitors."

"I hope you made them wipe their feet, I've only just finished polishing that floor!"

"Please excuse my wife, she's very proud of her home."
As he went behind his desk to sit, he muttered what
sounded like, "too damned proud if you ask me."

"Ok, fire away, who has died might help to clarify what
I might or might not know that could assist you."

"A lady you may have known by the name of Kitty
Brady."

Just at that moment a middle-aged woman entered the
room with the tray of tea, it now lay scattered and
shattered all over the beautiful, clean parquet floors.
She was ashen faced and was now holding herself
upright using the wing back chair Tam had previously
been sitting on.

"Oh, my dear, are you alright, what's wrong Mabel?"

"I'm so sorry, it was just hearing that ghastly woman's
name after all these years."

"Come and sit Mrs Fernie. So you knew the
deceased?"

"I know her name, yes."

Jack Fernie was now also ashen faced, "How do you know the name, Mabel?" his voice barely a whisper.

"Oh Jack, did you really think I wouldn't find out about your sordid lady friend? It must be almost thirteen years ago now, our youngest was about two, and I had not recovered well from his difficult birth and things were strained between us. I noticed, Jack... How you began sprucing yourself up and going out in the evenings more. Supposedly to the Seaforth's Club on the Mile. I knew, I just knew it was another woman. I got Rita Wilson, our neighbour in the house in Dudingston Mews, to babysit and I followed you. First to the club, I hoped, and I had almost convinced myself I'd been wrong when you came out with that woman on your arm. I followed you all the way to Marionville Road, and I saw you embrace and kiss her, before you went inside."

"The following day I went back there and presented myself as from the School Board doing checks on all the children registered in that area, I spoke to neighbours, and I was friendly. Have you any idea how these common women gossip?"

"Her husband was lost to her, but she wasn't having mine."

"Yet not a word to me about this, why didn't you confront me?" Jack reached and poured himself a large scotch.

"Soon after, not the next day, or the next week, but about three or so months on, you stopped suddenly, I was getting better, and our life resumed. My marriage was intact, my family was intact, and my heart and pride would mend in time. And it did, didn't it, we have been happy haven't we Jack?" Her voice held a desperate plea.

"Of course, dear girl, you know we have. I'm sorry Detective, this is a bit of a shock. As you might realise, I did have a brief affair with Kitty in 1935/36. She worked at the Seaforth Club. She was a widow. We got talking one night and I walked her home. It was a brief but intense bout of madness, which Kitty ended in the late summer of nineteen thirty-six. I've not seen or heard from her since."

"What happened to her Detective? How did she die?"

340

Before Jim had a chance to answer, Mabel interrupted, "Does it matter, what has this to do with my husband?"

"Well now, Mrs Fernie, Kitty was murdered!"

A breathless gasp escaped Jack Fernie as he clutched his chest, his face grey and sweaty. "Call 999 Mabel, NOW," said Tam.

Jim and Tam moved Jack to the floor and removed his tie and undid his collar. Mabel flew back into the room. "Jack, oh Jack, please, please don't die, don't leave me, I'm sorry, so sorry, I didn't mean it. I was just so hurt and angry. I found that receipt and certificate. I'm sorry, please my love, don't die."

She was inconsolable, her love for this man was obvious, but some of her remarks gave Jim Munro pause for thought. The ambulance arrived and Jack was whipped smartly off to the Royal Infirmary, his weeping wife in tow.

A week later, Jim sat at Jack's bedside. "Mr Fernie, I'm here to tell you that after your wife's visit in a moment I shall be formally arresting her. She will be charged with the third-degree murder of Kitty Brodie. It would seem the discovery of your daughter's birth certificate was the catalyst. She went to see Kitty that evening; only there did she learn of the child's death at three months. She also learnt that Kitty had broken it off with you in the wake of her loss. Seems she told your wife of your plans to leave your wife and family and move away with her and her boys."

"Your wife was confronted by the true depth of your betrayal, which made her years of hurt and sacrifice a mockery. That all that has been never really justified her silence. It felt as if it had all been a lie and she was only ever second best."

"Poor Kitty... Poor Mabel... what have I done?"

"Nothing against the Law of the Land, Mr Fernie. Only God's law was broken. I'm allowing this visit, so you best make your peace as best you can... Good-bye Mr Fernie."

Mabel was charged and convicted of third-degree murder and was sentenced to five years in jail. She forgave her husband and he has vowed to wait for her return.

Tam chapped on the door and poking his head round asked, "Sir, how did you know from the get-go that it was murder?"

"Well now Tam, Kitty was never seen without her hair brushed and her velluti cream on, and she'd have rather died than be seen with a ladder in her stocking. Also, the blood on the fender! There should have been a splatter pattern if she'd hit her head there. Yet everything was free of dust, not a spot, not even coal dross on the wee black lion."

"The wee lion, what's the relevance of that?"

James laughed, "As a lad I often witnessed Kitty use the lion to break a bigger lump of coal down. So it should have had coal dust on it."

"By Jings, velluti cream, a ladder and a fender all declared it a murder, but only in your eyes, sir."

"Yes, oh, and she'd never have answered the door with her pinny on. Night Tam."

The Ritual

In the year of Our Lord 1499, before the Spanish invaded, the Aztec city of Taxaco sat where modern-day Mexico City stands. A great and prosperous city and culture, where once a rich and lively people, lived, loved, and died. Here is the story of three young people from that ancient and sometimes brutal world.

Their names are:

Tizoc, his name means 'he has bled people', and is seventeen.

Quetzalli, her name means 'large, beautiful feather', she is from a noble family. She is sixteen

Chantico is her servant and friend, and her name means 'she who lives in the house'. She is fifteen.

Quetzalli thinks of Chantico as her friend, like a sister. They had been playmates since first Chantico had been stolen on a raid from a tribe from far away. Quetzalli's mother was dead and her father was often away in the wars. He kept Chantico as a servant companion for his daughter. They were of similar age and with no-one to monitor it, friendship grew in the midst of their isolation.

Tizoc was training to be a warrior. He was strong and handsome. Though a noble man, he was not of noble birth. He therefore hid his feelings for Quetzalli. He knew only pain awaited him on that path, but he had loved her for as long as he could remember.

His father was an aide to her father and they had played together in the courtyard of the large villa where she lived. Chantico knew Tizoc's heart. She saw it in every glance he stole when he believed no-one was watching. She also knew Quetzalli felt the same way. She also believed - like Tizoc - that only pain was waiting on that path.

Quetzalli was born into a high noble family and whilst she knew it to be a futile dream, she dreamt it nonetheless. She was destined to be a High Priestess; it was the stuff of her nightmares. To assist the High Priest in the sacrificial ceremonies, to see people she knew or not, die in such a way.

She often questioned the gods, why was the death of an innocent required to have a good crop, or rain or victory in war. Her people died of hunger even when offerings had been made.

She did not believe that the gods were interested in a swarm of locusts that would decimate a crop, and their young men died in the wars in equal numbers to their enemies.

She was punished often for such blasphemous thoughts, by her father and her tutor the high priest.

The success of the crops of corn, potatoes, beans, squashes and avocadoes grew or not, despite the offerings. Rain, sun, and good soil she believed had more relevance, than the offerings demanded by their priest's teachings. She would argue herself into another admonishment or more severe punishment on many occasions.

Her tutor's and her father's beatings taught her only one thing, to keep her opinions to herself. She must outwardly accede to their teachings.

She had plans of her own, and being a Priestess was not one of them. She was young, but she wasn't a complete ingenue, she'd seen Tizoc's secret looks.

The boy wore his heart on his face. She saw his dilemma and felt his distress, for she loved him in return. She had just learnt to hide her feelings. Only Chantico knew her secrets.

The night of the Rain Festival – in what we call February – was approaching. Quetzalli was determined to find Tizoc, to open her heart and reveal her plans to him. By the third festival of rain in August, she hoped to have fled Taxaco with Tizoc and Chantico forever.

A large bag of the gods' golden excrement would be saved and stored for the new life away from here. A traveller had passed a night visiting her father and she'd listened as he spoke of the power of the yellow metal and the greed of other nations to own it. She began to save these golden dung balls of the gods. They were hidden in a hole in the floor of her bedroom, beneath a heavy chest that held her ceremonial priestess robes.

All eyes were raised to the altar where the Priest and Quetzalli stood behind the ancient altar stone. Spreadeagled on the altar was a beautiful young black slave, taken in Honduras. His eyes showed the terror his paralysed body could not. The Priest was chanting his appeals to the gods, the obsidian dagger held aloft. The music was building to a massive drumming crescendo. When it peaked, in that first instant of silence, the dagger would tear into this poor soul's abdomen.

The Priest would, with the craft of a skilled butcher, remove his still beating heart. As a captive, his soul would not turn into the beautiful hummingbird; that was for great warriors or women who died in childbirth. His soul would be damned – or so they were told by the High Priest. Quetzalli stilled the fierce urge to run; she must appear compliant tonight.

When all was done, Quetzalli found Tizoc talking with Chantico by the fountain. Chantico was aware of tonight's importance to her friend and so begged leave to get her mistress some food. Quetzalli moved into the shadow beside the great stairs and beneath one of the great statues that stood like giant sentinels on either side of the steps. She was not a shy girl and so wasted no time.

"Tizoc, please do not interrupt me till I have finished, if I am wrong in my beliefs, then please just walk away without a word, and I will speak of this no more. I have lost my heart to you. I know the danger it brings with it. I also believe you feel the same way. If I am wrong, go now, say nothing, just go."

She looked up into the face of the man she loved. His face was lit in a way she'd never seen before, his love for her shone like a fiery beacon.

"Tezico, if you are willing to risk all - as I am -we have plans to make. I will offer my life gladly for a single day of freedom where I can love you in the light. Tell me your mind."

He hesitated, then replied, "Not tonight, we will find ways to meet and talk and plan, but not now, not here. Go, drink with your friends, feast and sleep then in the warmth of my love."

Over the months they met and planned and secreted away the golden nuggets. Chantico dried meats from wild turkey, rabbit and snake for their journey, it was stashed in one of the old storerooms. There were clothes as well, all stored ready for the approaching third festival of rain.

Quetzalli's father returned from his most recent expedition, bringing more slaves taken from the indigenous peoples of what in the future would become Costa Rica and Guatemala. The three conspirators believed no-one had noticed anything untoward from the triumvirate. They were wrong.

Atzi was next in line for the position of High Priestess, a substitute if you will, in case Quetzalli didn't reach maturity. Atzi was devout and devoted all her time to the teachings and was happy to assist the Priest in any ceremony. She longed for the position that Quetzalli questioned like a heretic. She had shadowed Quetzalli since long before the night of the Rain Festival when Tizoc and Quetzalli had declared themselves.

When things subtly changed, it was not missed by the eagle-eye of Quetzalli's unknown enemy. Atzi had seen her rival become more cautious, so she stayed in the shadows, and missed nothing, She was an intelligent girl; she spied on the two other players in this drama, a drama she was certain would unfold and deliver her into the position she desired so badly.

Chantico had packed all the food, along with rudimentary cooking utensils and had wrapped it in extra garments for her mistress. All was ready for the night three days hence.

An old sailor had provided them with a basic map of the area north of the Acequia Madre river. Beyond there was dangerous territory, inhabited by Apache, Tonawa and Comanche peoples, fierce and warlike peoples, who - like her own - took slaves. Hopefully the map would help lead them safely to freedom and a new life.

Quetzalli slipped out of the walled courtyard and into the orchard beyond, staying in the combined shadows of the trees and the wall. There she found Tizoc waiting. They embraced and the kiss they shared was all Atzi needed. She could discredit Quetzalli, challenging her chastity, for the Priestess must be chaste and pure. This kiss destroyed any claim Quetzalli might argue. That and the evidence in the cache of food, clothes and the map would also implicate the lover and friend. Her path would be clear, and she could destroy the girl she so hated.

Without warning, the guards stormed the home of Quetzalli. Tizoc was arrested at the Men's Hall where the warriors in training lived.

Brought before a Council on the eve of the Rain Festival, the charges and evidence were presented and Atzi's testament heard. The three stood before the people, tied and guarded. Their guilt was decided. They were not permitted to speak. Dawn would bring the decision of the Council and they would learn their fate.

The High Priest, who had always detested this wilful girl, demanded the traitors and the whore be offered to the Gods that night. His argument of the triple sacrifice was a powerful one as the summer had been very dry, the last crop yield was desperately needed to see them through the hard times to come. The Council voted, some voices called for mercy at least for Chantico, who should be seen as only doing her mistress's bidding. Those voices went unheard. All three were sentenced to be offered to the Gods of rain later that day.

The trio were held together in a storage hut near the square. They huddled together, Tizoc held Quetzalli close and spoke softly to her, vainly attempting to comfort her. His heart was breaking, his powerlessness to save this woman who held his heart, was too much for any man to bear.

Quetzalli's father was permitted late in the afternoon to visit his only child. With a broken heart he embraced his daughter, who so reminded him of her mother. As he pulled away, he pressed a small packet into her hands. He embraced her again, whispering in her ear, "It's all I can do for you, put it in the water jug. It's swift, the pain short lived. Goodbye daughter, and may the gods have mercy on you."

After he left, Quetzalli opened the packet and showed it to Tizoc. He nodded and tipped its content into the water gourd, pouring three cups. As Quetzalli took hers and Chantico's cup, the guards entered.

Tizoc, in an effort to give the girls a chance to drink, charged the door. Quetzalli understood his selfless act and bade Chantico to drink, quickly, she held the hands and the eye of her dearest friend. By the time the guards had Tizoc subdued, both girls lay dead on the floor, their fingers entwined in a claw like grip. Tizoc was relieved to know his beautiful Quetzalli would not face the obsidian dagger. His ritual offering would be all that the Gods would get tonight.

He walked up the steps to the altar, the rope about his neck meant nothing. In his mind's eye, he could see her, waiting, standing to the side of the altar. As he lay on the large altar stone, he focused on her image in his mind. His eyes locked on hers and he didn't see the ancient dagger fall; the momentary pain passed as he left his body and joined his love.

Three hummingbirds flew overhead, free.

Image by Gordon Johnson, from Pixabay

The Stormy Sea

It is the year of Our Lord sixteen fifty. The *Silhouette*, a three-masted wooden sailing ship was loading on the docks of Bristol, on England's southwest coast. Most sailors aboard were out of sorts and ill-tempered, having either been tricked or press-ganged, due to drunkenness or debts, into signing on for this voyage.

They sang as they heaved the cargo of woollen textiles, copper, guns, and munitions aboard, and set them in the hold. The twelve-month voyage was not one that most of these tars looked forward to as the *Silhouette* slipped her moorings and set sail for warmer climes.

Sierra Leone.

Ishmael had seen fifteen summers, considered a man in his village. He'd endured the challenges and tasks each boy must undertake before he may wear the mark of warrior and a man. Ishmael's father, Kossi, had schooled him well, yet lovingly. Many of his friend's fathers were hard and brutal in their quest to make men of their sons. The tribe depended on the abilities of the young to provide for the village. Warriors and hunters were revered: they were the future of their people.

Only yesterday his father had taken Ishmael aside and warned him to be extra vigilant when they were away from their tribal lands. He had met a traveller who regaled Kossi with tales of great beasts of ships and men who killed, raped, and destroyed the villages north of here, and worse - they stole the healthy young men and women away in the ships. Ishmael heard the words of his father but dismissed them as the imaginings and exaggerations of old women. He'd heard these horror stories before but were about isolated incidents in Senegal.

Kobi and Ishmael had been friends all their lives. They did everything together and today they were in the brush stalking a large fat Bongo whose meat was a favourite of their village. This catch would earn them kudos as hunters. Just as they moved to close their trap, they were suddenly brought to ground by giant nets. The hunters had been hunted and were caught fast. But by whom, Ishmael pondered, a local tribe they had disputes with, or the white people stealers? His worst fears were realised a moment or two later when a dozen or more men appeared.

They were shackled to each other, then led down to the inlet where a small vessel waited, it would take them out to the enormous barque sitting in the bay at the mouth of the great Bumpe River. Sitting in chains on the beach were about one hundred men and women about their ages, or a little older.

As they reached the group, one of their captors unlocked Kobi's shackle and in the instant before the new cuff was fixed, Kobi bucked, causing the shackle to fall. He bolted.

Kobi was like the leopard, fast and lithe, but as he crested the dunes, several slavers raised their muskets and fired. Ishmael had shouted a warning, but too late. Kobi was dead, the bullet from a slaver's gun had hit him in the head. The damage was devastating and deadly.

Ishmael dropped into a crouch and charged one of the killers of his dearest friend. He wanted the stinking, filthy slaver to know his own death. The butt of the slaver's gun dropped him on the spot. He awoke in chains in the belly of the ship.

The smell was nauseating. Fouling what little air afforded them was the odour of unwashed bodies, of body fluids and the dead. Some had clearly passed more than a week before. However, it was neither the smell nor the noise of nearly six hundred souls that roused him, the ship was being tossed like a cork in a barrel.

Suddenly there was a thunderous crack and a cry from above, an instant later the deck above their heads was split wide open. One of the masts had been felled by the force of the cyclone raging above. A sailor had been caught in the masts' crash through the hull and lay over Ishmaels legs, and Allah be praised, there hung on his belt a set of keys. The boy opposite him used his free foot to pick them up and sent them sailing into Ishmael's lap. Within minutes there were about one hundred men and women racing to free the living and heading for the top deck, just in time to see the slavers launching their row boats.

The mast had penetrated the hull below the water line. The ship was sinking.

Ishmael could see the coast. He held his nerve till the barque finally shuddered and heaved its last, then he pushed away and swam hard for the shoreline. This terrible storm would decide if he travelled to the arms of Allah or the arms of his mother and family. Only God knew which, but he was strong and determined to live to avenge his friend.

Image from OpenClipArt-Vectors on Pixabay

Photo of Gabriel Baird Carmichael with his fiancee', Christine,
before returning to France in World War I

From the author's personal collection

Acknowledgements

My mother, Anne Merville Donoghue, was the niece of Private Gabriel Baird Carmichael. It was curiosity regarding her middle name, after the town in northern France where Gabriel's last missive was posted, that first piqued my interest in World War I.

My love of books was born through my Nana, Catherine Donoghue (nee Tierney), who taught me to read before I started school and enrolled me at the local library. My father, Joseph Donoghue, fired and inspired my imagination through his story-telling; his wonderful, fanciful stories included how he fought with Custer at Little Bighorn and with Hannibal as he crossed the Alps. All writers need encouragement, and I got that from my English teacher, Mr. Whiteside, at St. Richards RC School in Bexhill.

More recently, I have to thank my oldest friend, Diane Massey, who always reads my stuff and encourages me to do more. Others too numerous to mention have seen my scribblings on social media, but especially Jean Arnott and her husband, Billy (who, sadly, is no longer with us), who loved my tales and would read my stories while on holiday.

Then there are the people of the now... Elizabeth and Lisa Talbott, who have at times caused me to blush and at other times cry in the wake of their praise and encouragement. Indeed, Lisa helped me prepare this book as a proof-reader. But more than that, she introduced my work to her publisher and was instrumental in getting this book into his hands.

I also have to recognize Michael Paul Hurd, an author in his own right and owner of Lineage Independent Publishing. He believed my words are worthy of the paper they are printed on and that the stories in this book will touch you in some way.

To my beautiful children, Andrew, Nesrin, and Jem: the biggest thank you! Without you, I would never have become the me of today: a published author.

To all who I have named here and many more besides who have helped me become the person who could do this, thank you from the bottom of my heart.

I hope you have enjoyed the journey through my imaginings of love, murder, history, war, and redemption. More importantly, I hope that my characters were real enough that you were part of the story.

Patricia Carmichael / G.B. Donoghue

Lightning Source UK Ltd.
Milton Keynes UK
UKHW010654160921
390678UK00003B/504